A New Dawn

America Series, Volume 3

William Myers

Published by William Myers, 2024.

This is a work of fiction. Similarities to real people, places, or events are entirely coincidental.

A NEW DAWN

First edition. August 29, 2024.

Copyright © 2024 William Myers.

ISBN: 979-8227171863

Written by William Myers.

Dedicated to President Trump and all those who are conservative in their stance.

LET FREEDOM RING: The dawn of redemption

The Final Book by William G. Myers

29 AUGUST 2024

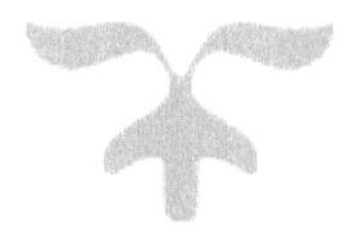

INTRODUCTION

Introduction to the Final Book: The Dawn of a New America

As the sun dipped below the horizon, casting long shadows across the desolate landscape, General William Shepard stood on the deck of the USS Liberty, gazing out at the waters that had once been the lifeblood of a free nation. The war that had torn through the heart of America was entering its final phase, and the weight of all that had come before weighed heavily on his shoulders.

Book 1: The Invasion Begins

The first book in this series, *The Invasion Begins*, opened with a nightmare scenario: a coordinated invasion of the United States by a coalition of Russian, Chinese, and North Korean forces. The initial shock was overwhelming. Major cities fell, communication networks were crippled, and the military, caught off guard, struggled to mount a cohesive defense.

It was in these darkest hours that the seeds of New America were planted. General Shepard, then a Colonel, rallied the remnants of his forces and began a desperate campaign of resistance. The odds were stacked against them, but Shepard knew that giving up was not an option. The story followed the harrowing experiences of soldiers and civilians alike as they navigated a world turned upside down. From the destruction of Washington D.C. to the daring escapes from occupied territories, *The Invasion Begins* was a tale of survival, defiance, and the indomitable spirit of a people who refused to surrender.

Key characters were introduced, including Colonel James Williams, who would go on to lead the 2nd Armoured Division in some of the war's most critical battles. The first book ended with a glimmer of hope: the formation of New America, a nation born from the ashes of the old, united by a common purpose—to reclaim their homeland and restore freedom to their people.

By close examination, New America consisted of 30 states, but it fell to twenty because of the enemy's superiority. The lack of leadership led to the easy takeover of the ten.

Book 2: The Resistance Rises

It infuriated the citizens of New America after the last ten states were conquered. Oppressed America was up to thirty states.

An invisible line separated Brothers and sisters and mothers and fathers. And fear and executions kept the populace in check.

The Resistance Rises

The story shifts focus from survival to organized resistance. New America, under the leadership of General Shepard and a newly formed national committee, began to mount a series of counterattacks. The military strategy was clear: divide and conquer. By targeting supply lines, communication hubs, and critical enemy strongholds, New America's forces slowly began to turn the tide.

This book introduced new characters and expanded the scope of the conflict. We followed the harrowing covert missions of Captain Jim Jordan and his Green Berets as they struck deep behind enemy lines, freeing prisoners and sabotaging enemy operations. We saw the rise of Colonel Blake Dill and his band of guerrilla fighters, who became a thorn in the side of the occupying forces, launching daring raids from their hidden bases.

But *The Resistance Rises* was a tale of military might and the human cost of war. The psychological toll on soldiers and civilians alike was explored in depth. Families were torn apart, communities were destroyed, and the constant fear of death weighed heavily on everyone. Yet, amid the despair, there were moments of courage and hope. The book ended with a decisive victory at the Battle of the Great Plains, a turning point that marked the beginning of the end for the invaders.

Setting the Stage for the Final Book

As the final book begins, New America stands on the brink of ultimate victory. The invading forces are in disarray, their supply lines cut, and their morale shattered. But the war is not over. The enemy, though weakened, is still dangerous, and the final push to drive them out of American soil will be the most challenging yet.

New America's forces have grown more vigorous in numbers and resolve. The once ragtag army of survivors has become a formidable military force, hardened by years of relentless combat. Yet, the challenges ahead are daunting. The enemy's leaders, driven by a desire for revenge, plan one last desperate counteroffensive. In the face of this new threat, the unity of New America will be tested as never before.

Themes and Motifs

This saga's final chapter will explore the enduring themes woven throughout the series: resilience, sacrifice, patriotism, and faith. The American flag, Old Glory, which has flown over countless battlefields, remains a potent symbol of hope and defiance. It represents not just the land but the ideals that define a nation—freedom, democracy, and the unyielding belief in a better future.

The characters who have carried the story so far will continue their journeys, facing new challenges and making decisions that will shape the future of New America. The theme of leadership will be central, as those in command must navigate the fine line between victory and disaster. The sacrifices made along the way will not be forgotten, and the final book will pay tribute to the men and women who gave everything for their country.

Character Arcs

Now, the leader of New America's military, General Shepard, has been through hell and back. His journey from a battle-weary soldier to a revered leader has been marked by moments of doubt, loss, and incredible courage. As the final book begins, Shepard must confront the reality of what it means to lead a nation in war. His decisions will determine the fate of millions, and the weight of that responsibility will push him to his limits.

Colonel James Williams, the commander of the 2nd Armoured Division, has emerged as one of the most capable and respected officers in New America's military. His tactical brilliance and unyielding resolve have won him the loyalty of his troops, but the battles ahead will test his leadership as never before. Williams will face choices that challenge his beliefs and force him to confront the cost of victory.

Captain Jim Jordan, the leader of the Green Berets, has become a symbol of the resistance—a man willing to risk everything for the cause. His covert operations have been instrumental in turning the tide of the war, but the final mission he undertakes will be his most dangerous yet. Jordan's story will explore the personal toll of war as he grapples with the loss of comrades and the weight of his own survival.

Explanation of the Story So Far

The first two books of this series have taken readers on a journey through a world torn apart by war. The invasion that shattered the United States was a catastrophe of unimaginable proportions, but it also sparked a new beginning. New America, forged in the crucible of conflict, has emerged as a beacon of hope in a world plunged into darkness.

The timeline of events has been marked by key battles and strategic decisions that have shaped the course of the war. From the fall of

Washington D.C. to the decisive victory at the Battle of the Great Plains, each moment has brought New America closer to reclaiming its lost territory. Establishing a new government, led by a national committee, has provided the structure needed to unite the people and coordinate the war effort.

Throughout this journey, the characters have faced moral and ethical dilemmas that have tested their resolve. Decisions made in the heat of battle have had far-reaching consequences, both for the individuals involved and the nation. As the final book begins, the story has reached a critical juncture. The enemy is on the run but still needs to be defeated. The final showdown will ultimately test New America's strength and determination.

Foreshadowing the Final Confrontation

The final book will bring all the story threads together in a climactic confrontation that will determine the future of New America. The enemy, though weakened, has not given up. They are planning one last, desperate offensive to regain their lost foothold. But New America is ready. The lessons learned in the fires of war have prepared them for this moment.

New threats will emerge, and unresolved conflicts will come to the fore. The final book will challenge the characters in ways they never imagined, pushing them to their limits and forcing them to confront the true cost of victory. The stakes have never been higher, and the outcome is still being determined. But one thing is clear: New America will not go quietly into the night. The fight for freedom, for the very soul of a nation, is about to reach its epic conclusion.

LET FREEDOM RING: The dawn of redemption

The room was dimly lit, with the only light coming from a massive screen displaying a detailed map of the Americas. Around the table sat the most powerful men and women in New America, each with a crucial role to play: James Alexander, Chair of the National Committee; the strategist; General of the Army, Command Sergeant Major turned General, the tactician; Admiral Jim Beasley, the executor; and the now highly respected Colonel Blake Dill, the negotiator. In the corner, quietly observing, was Brother Michael, a spiritual advisor to the committee, who had become a symbol of hope and moral guidance for the nation.

James Alexander stood at the head of the table, his sharp eyes scanning the faces of his comrades. The room buzzed with tension, anticipation, and a sense of unity. This meeting had been long in the making, and the time had come to execute a plan that would change the course of history.

James Alexander: "Ladies and gentlemen, the time has come. We've been fighting a long, hard war. We've taken hits, but we've given even harder ones. Now, it's time to deliver the final blow that will push these invaders out of our land once and for all." His words, filled with courage and determination, inspired hope in the hearts of his comrades.

The General of the Army leaned forward, his jaw set in unyielding determination. **"We've been preparing for this for years. The enemy's control has weakened, but their grip is still strong in key areas. We must hit them where it hurts most to break it—at the top." His words were a testament to the unwavering determination of the New American forces.**

Admiral Jim Beasley: "You're talking about the leadership. If we can remove the heads of their government, we can throw their entire operation into chaos." His words hung in the air, carrying the weight of the potential impact of their mission and the suspense of the outcome.

James Alexander: "Precisely. The plan is straightforward, but it will require precision and coordination on an unprecedented scale. We will launch a series of covert operations to kidnap or eliminate key political figures in the Russian, Chinese, and North Korean governments who are stationed in the Americas."

Colonel Blake Dill: "This won't be easy. These leaders are surrounded by security forces, heavily guarded, and constantly on the move. But if we can take them, we'll have the leverage to negotiate their withdrawal." The daunting nature of the mission hung in the air, adding to the suspense and anticipation.

General of the Army nodded, his eyes cold and calculating. "This isn't just about taking them out. It's about sending a message. We won't negotiate with these invaders; we'll make them realize that their hold on our country is untenable."

James Alexander: "We'll deploy our best teams—those who have proven themselves in the field, who know how to get in and out without a trace. Colonel Dill, your 'Shake and Bake' operation has shown us that it's possible to strike fear into the enemy's heart. We need that same level of ferocity and precision."

Colonel Dill, ever the strategist, leaned back, considering the plan. "We'll need to coordinate this across multiple theaters, striking simultaneously. We can't give them time to react. My men are ready, but we'll need intelligence—exact locations, movements, habits of these targets."

Admiral Beasley glanced at the map. "Our stealth ships, equipped with the latest technology, are strategically positioned. We can use them to insert teams close to the targets. Air support will be limited to avoid detection, but we can provide extraction points along the coast."

Brother Michael, who had remained silent until now, spoke up, his voice calm but resolute. "**This plan is bold, and it carries great risk. We must remember that we fight not just for victory but for the soul of our nation. Let our actions be guided by righteousness, even in the face of such peril.**"

James Alexander: "We all know the stakes. We've seen the devastation these invaders have brought to our homeland, and we've seen the resolve of our people to take it back. This is our chance to end this war, to restore our freedom and sovereignty."

General of the Army looked around the table, meeting each person's eyes. "**Then it's settled. We'll move forward with the plan. But remember, this is an all-or-nothing operation. There's no room for error.**"

The room fell into a contemplative silence as each person considered the weight of what was to come. Then, one by one, they nodded in agreement.

Colonel Blake Dill: "I'll begin preparing my men immediately. We'll need a week to finalize our plans and deploy."

Admiral Beasley: "I'll ensure the naval forces are in position and ready to provide support. We'll be in constant communication, but once the operation begins, we'll go dark."

Brother Michael: "I'll pray for the success of this mission and the safety of all those involved. Our faith has carried us this far and will continue to guide us."

James Alexander: "Good. Let's make history, people. For New America."

The room was filled with tense energy as the leaders of New America gathered to finalize their most ambitious plan. The large screen in front of them displayed the mission details, with each team's objective highlighted in bold.

James Alexander, the Chair of the National Committee, stood at the head of the table. His voice was steady, filled with resolve. "**The time has come to drive the Russians, Chinese, and North Koreans out of the Americas once and for all. We've spent years perfecting our operations and must execute them flawlessly. Our enemies think they are invincible, but they've made a grave mistake by underestimating our resolve.**"

General of the Army, once a Command Sergeant Major of the 101st Airborne Division, leaned forward. "**We're ready, Mr. Chair. The Navy SEALs have been training for this mission for years. They're prepared to infiltrate North Korea and capture their leader. We'll take away the head of the snake and leave their forces in disarray.**"

Admiral Jim Beasley nodded in agreement, commanding the bulk of New America's naval forces. "**Our SEALs are the best in the world. They know the stakes and are fully aware of the risks. Once the North Korean leader is in our custody, the psychological blow to their forces will be immense. Their morale will crumble.**"

James Alexander turned his attention to Colonel Blake Dill, who had become legendary for his guerrilla warfare against the invaders. "**Colonel, the Rangers have an equally critical mission. They'll be tasked with abducting the Russian President and key figures from the Kremlin. We need them to understand that their presence in the Americas is no longer tenable.**"

Colonel Dill, a man of few words, nodded. "**The Rangers are ready. We'll hit them where it hurts. They won't know what hit them until it's too late.**"

Brother Michael, who had been quietly observing from the corner of the room, spoke up. "**These missions will require more than just skill and courage. Our men will need to be guided by something greater. This is not just a battle for territory; it's a battle for the soul of our nation. We must pray for their success.**"

General Alexander nodded with appreciation before continuing. "Finally, the Green Berets. They've been assigned the task of kidnapping the Chinese leader. This mission is perhaps the most dangerous of all, given the proximity to the Chinese mainland. But we have confidence in their abilities. They've trained for this moment, and they're ready to carry it out."

Admiral Beasley added, "Once these leaders are in our custody, we'll have the leverage to force their withdrawal from the Americas. The world will see that we are no longer a nation on the defensive. We're taking the fight to them."

James Alexander stood, signaling the end of the briefing. "This is the moment we've been preparing for. Our freedom, our way of life, depends on the success of these missions. May God be with every one of our soldiers."

As the leaders dispersed to finalize preparations, the task's weight settled over them. The missions would require precision, bravery, and an unshakable resolve. But they knew this was the only way to secure their future.

Days Later, on the Ground In North Korea

Eighty Miles off the Coast of North Korea

Admiral Jim Beasley stood tall on the flagship's deck, the wind whipping around him as the vast expanse of the Pacific Ocean stretched out in all directions. The sun began to dip below the horizon, casting a golden hue across the water. Before him, rows of sailors, Marines, and SEALs stood at attention, their eyes fixed on their leader. The air was thick with anticipation as they prepared for the most significant mission of their lives.

"Men, I want you to take a moment to look around," Admiral Beasley began, his voice strong and resonant, carrying across the deck. **"Look at this vast ocean, the sun setting over the water. This is what we fight for—the freedom to stand on this deck, under this sky, and know that we are free men and women. Decades ago, our ancestors did the impossible. They stood up against an oppressive empire, an empire that sought to crush their spirits and dictate their lives. Against impossible odds, they rose and created a nation where liberty was more than just a word—it was a way of life."**

He paused, letting the weight of his words settle over his men. **"They fought for a dream, a vision of a land where every person could live without fear, speak their minds, worship as they chose, and raise their families in peace. That dream wasn't handed to them; they bled for it and sacrificed everything. And today, we find ourselves at a similar crossroads."**

The Admiral's gaze swept over the assembled forces; his eyes filled with resolve. **"For years, we have been pushed back, cornered, and forced to watch as foreign powers trampled on the very soil that our forefathers fought so hard to protect. But we never gave up. We retreated, but only to regroup, strengthen, and become the force you see standing here today. We are on the precipice of winning** back what we have lost. We are the sons and daughters of that same spirit, and that unbreakable resolve forged a nation out of tyranny. And today, we carry that legacy forward."

He took a step forward, his voice growing even more powerful. "This is more than just a battle for land or power. This is a battle for the soul of our nation. Our enemies have taken much from us but could never take our spirit or will to fight for what is rightfully ours. We stand here today not just as soldiers, sailors, or SEALs but as Americans. We are the torchbearers of liberty, the defenders of freedom. Our mission is clear: we will reclaim our land, people, and future."

Admiral Beasley raised his fist in the air, symbolizing unity and strength. "We will not falter. We will not retreat. Our enemies believe they have the upper hand and have broken us. But they are gravely mistaken. Today, we will show them the true power of a united and determined people. Today, we begin the march toward victory and a free and united America once more."

The men and women before him straightened, their hearts swelling with pride and determination. They were ready—ready to fight, prepared to sacrifice, ready to reclaim the freedom that had been stolen from them. As the sun dipped below the horizon, casting the fleet in shadow, they knew that tomorrow would bring the dawn of a new era that they would forge with their hands.

Admiral Beasley's voice rang out one last time. "Let's write the next chapter of American history together. Let's show the world what it means to be free. For our families, our fallen, and our future—let's bring them home."

With a resounding cheer, the men and women of the fleet responded, their voices echoing across the waters. The time had come to reclaim their destiny.

In the Shadows

The moon hung low in the night sky, casting a pale glow over North Korea's rugged terrain. The Navy SEALs moved with the precision and discipline that had been drilled into them over years of training and countless missions. Each step was calculated, and every breath was measured. They were ghosts in the darkness, unseen and unheard but with an undeniable presence.

The landscape around them was unforgiving—rocky outcroppings, dense forests, and narrow paths that twisted and turned unpredictably. But the SEALs navigated it all with ease. They studied satellite images, memorized the terrain, and practiced this mission in simulations until it was second nature. Now, the time had come to put all that preparation into action.

Ahead of them, the North Korean leader's compound loomed like a fortress in the night, its high walls topped with razor wire and guard towers standing sentry at each corner. The compound was heavily fortified, but the SEALs knew no fortress was impenetrable. They had studied every weak point and vulnerability and were ready to exploit them.

The team leader, a seasoned veteran with years of covert operations under his belt, paused for a moment to assess the situation. Through his night-vision goggles, he could see the guards' patrol patterns, the infrared beams crisscrossing the entrance, and the cameras scanning the perimeter. His team was in position, crouched low and waiting for his signal.

He whispered the final command into his radio, his voice barely more than a breath. "**On my mark... go.**"

With that, the SEALs sprang into action. They moved with lethal efficiency, their silenced weapons taking down the guards before they could react. The first guard fell silently, a dart from a tranquilizer gun hitting him in the neck. He crumpled to the ground without a sound.

Another guard was neutralized with a swift strike to the throat, his body caught by a SEAL before it could hit the ground.

The team moved in perfect synchronization, each member knowing their role in the letter. They split into two groups—one to disable the compound's security systems and the other to secure the main entrance. The SEALs tasked with disabling the security moved swiftly to the control room. They bypassed the electronic locks and deactivated the alarm systems, rendering the compound's defensess useless.

The second team breached the main gate, their cutting-edge tools slicing through the heavy steel locks as if they were made of paper. Once inside, they continued their advance, systematically clearing each room they passed. They left no trace of their presence—no alarms, gunfire, or sign that anything was amiss.

As they neared the inner sanctum, the tension mounted. They knew that the North Korean leader would be surrounded by his most loyal and heavily armed guards. But the SEALs were undeterred. They had trained for this very scenario and were ready for whatever awaited them.

The inner sanctum was a stark contrast to the rest of the compound. It was opulent, with marble floors, ornate furnishings, and priceless artwork adorning the walls. But the SEALs had no time to admire the surroundings. They moved quickly and quietly, their senses heightened, ready for any threat.

The team leader signaled his men to prepare for entry as they reached the final door. They stacked up on either side of the door, weapons ready. The leader placed a small explosive charge on the lock and stepped back. The charge detonated with a muffled pop, and the door swung open.

The SEALs moved in; their weapons trained on the room's occupants. The North Korean leader was there, surrounded by his guards. But the guards were no match for the Seals' speed and precision. Within seconds, they were neutralized, their weapons knocked from their hands, their bodies incapacitated by expertly placed blows.

The North Korean leader, wide-eyed and terrified, backed into a corner, his hands raised in surrender. The SEAL team leader approached him, his voice cold and commanding. **"It's over. You're coming with us."**

The leader was subdued and secured, his hands bound, and his mouth gagged to prevent him from calling out. The SEALs moved swiftly, extracting him from the compound with the same precision they had used to enter. They retraced their steps, avoiding detection as they returned to the extraction point.

As they reached the waiting helicopter, the SEAL team leader took one last look at the compound, now silent and undisturbed, as if nothing had happened. The mission had been executed flawlessly. The North Korean leader was in their custody, and the SEALs were on their way to deliver him to New America.

As the helicopter lifted off, the team allowed themselves a moment of satisfaction. They had done what many believed impossible, striking at the heart of the enemy's leadership without leaving a trace. They were the best, and tonight they had again proven it.

In Russia

The cold night air bit at the faces of the Rangers as they descended silently through the sky, the only sounds being the faint rustle of parachutes and the distant howl of the wind. They were miles from their drop zone, deep behind enemy lines in the heart of Russia. The moonlight barely penetrated the thick cloud cover, casting a muted glow over the landscape below. Each Ranger was focused, every movement precise as they guided their parachutes toward the target—a remote clearing outside the city.

This was no ordinary mission. They were tasked with abducting the Russian President and key Kremlin officials during a high-security meeting, an operation that would send shockwaves around the world. The stakes were as high as possible, and failure was not an option.

On the Ground

As they touched down in the snow-covered clearing, the Rangers swiftly gathered their gear, packed their parachutes, and moved into formation. The team leader, Captain Jason Rivers, signaled for radio silence as they trek through the dense forest surrounding the Kremlin compound.

"Eyes sharp, men," Captain Rivers whispered into his comm. **"We've trained for this. Stick to the plan, and we'll be in and out before they know we're there."**

The Rangers moved with the precision of a well-oiled machine, their footsteps barely making a sound as they navigated the rugged terrain. They had spent weeks studying every detail of the Kremlin's defensess, from patrol routes to electronic surveillance systems. Tonight, all that preparation would be put to the test.

The team paused to assess the situation as they approached the Kremlin compound's perimeter. The compound was a fortress surrounded by high walls, security cameras, and heavily armed guards. But the Rangers had one advantage—they knew exactly where to strike.

"Alpha team, you're on overwatch," Captain Rivers ordered. **"Bravo team, with me. We're going in hot."**

The Infiltration

The Alpha team moved into position on a ridge overlooking the compound, setting up their sniper rifles and monitoring the guards' movements. The Bravo team, led by Captain Rivers, began their approach, using the shadows and blind spots in the compound's defensess to their advantage.

"Guard at ten o'clock," whispered Sergeant Harris, the team's sharpshooter, as he sighted in on a lone sentry patrolling the perimeter. With a nod from Captain Rivers, Harris squeezed the trigger, and the sentry crumpled silently to the ground. Another guard met the same fate moments later, allowing the Rangers to slip through the outer defenses undetected.

They reached the compound's wall and quickly set up a rope ladder. The Rangers scaled the wall one by one, their movements fluid and practiced. Once inside, they split into two groups—one to disable the security systems, the other to breach the meeting room where the President and Kremlin officials were gathered.

Corporal Davis, the team's tech expert, worked quickly to hack into the security feed. **"We're in,"** he whispered, his fingers flying over the keyboard. **"Cameras are on a loop. We've got ten minutes before the system resets."**

Captain Rivers nodded, signaling for the breach. The Rangers moved swiftly through the corridors, their weapons at the ready. They encountered no resistance as they closed in on the high-security meeting room. The Kremlin officials were unaware of the danger lurking just outside their door.

The Breach

Captain Rivers held up three fingers, counting down silently. Three... two... one. The door to the meeting room burst open with a loud crash as the Rangers stormed in, weapons drawn, lasers trained on the stunned officials. The room was filled with a tense silence as the occupants froze, their eyes wide with shock and fear.

Accustomed to absolute control, the Russian President was momentarily paralyzed with disbelief. This was the heart of Russian power, the most secure room in the country, and yet these American soldiers had breached it with ease.

Captain Rivers locked eyes with the President, his voice cold and commanding. **"You're coming with us. Don't make this harder than it needs to be."**

The President's guards reached for weapons, but the Rangers were faster. In a blur of motion, the guards were disarmed and subdued, leaving the President and his officials defenseless. The Rangers moved with ruthless efficiency, binding the hands of the President and the key Kremlin officials with zip ties.

"Who do you think you are?" the President spat, his voice trembling with anger and fear.

"We're the reckoning," Captain Rivers replied, his voice as steady as a rock. **"Now, move."**

Stunned and terrified, the officials offered no resistance as they were herded out of the room. The Rangers maintained their tight formation, keeping their weapons trained on the captives as they moved quickly through the compound.

Corporal Davis's voice crackled over the comms. **"System's about to reset. We need to be out in sixty seconds."**

"Copy that," Captain Rivers replied. **"Alpha team, we're extracting. Get ready."**

The Extraction

The Rangers moved swiftly through the compound, their captives in tow. They reached the outer wall, where the rope ladder was still in place. One by one, they climbed down, guiding the captives as they descended. The extraction point was less than a mile away, a heavily forested area where their helicopter awaited.

As they reached the extraction point, the sound of rotor blades slicing through the air grew louder. The Rangers hustled their captives into the waiting helicopter, securing them for the flight out. Captain Rivers took one last look at the Kremlin, now fading into the distance, before climbing aboard.

The helicopter lifted off, the downdraft from the rotors kicking up a snow cloud. Inside, the Rangers remained alert, their weapons still trained on the captives. The President stared at Captain Rivers, his expression a mix of fury and disbelief.

"This isn't over," the President growled.

Captain Rivers met his gaze without flinching. **"It is for you."**

As the helicopter sped away, the Rangers knew they had just struck a devastating blow to the heart of their enemy. They had accomplished the impossible, capturing the most powerful man in Russia, deep within his territory, without losing a single man. The mission was successful, but they knew this was just the beginning. The war for America's future was far from over, but tonight, they had taken a giant step toward victory.

In China

The Green Berets had trained for missions like this their entire careers, but none had been as daunting as the one before them. The Chinese leader's compound was a veritable fortress, surrounded by layers of advanced security measures, elite guards, and impenetrable walls. Many considered the mission nearly impossible, but the Green Berets knew failure was not an option. They were the best and would not stop until their objective was complete.

The Approach

The team had infiltrated deep into Chinese territory, moving under darkness. They navigated treacherous terrain, avoiding detection from drones and patrols. Their approach was gruelling through dense forests, jagged mountains, and fast-moving rivers. Every step was dangerous, but the Green Berets moved with unwavering determination.

Captain Jim Jordan, the team leader, crouched low as he observed the compound through his binoculars. The massive walls were topped with barbed wire, and guard towers were strategically placed along the perimeter. Floodlights illuminated the area, and motion detectors scanned for any sign of movement.

"We've got a tough nut to crack here, boys," Captain Jordan whispered into his comms. **"But we've faced worse. Remember, this isn't just a mission—it's the final blow. We take him, and we start turning the tide."**

Staff Sergeant Kyle Turner, the team's demolitions expert, grinned as he double-checked his gear. **"I've cracked tougher, sir. Just point me at where you want the hole."**

Corporal Danny "Doc" Ramirez, the team medic, chimed in, his voice calm despite the tension. **"Let's just make sure we all get out of here in one piece. I've got no plans to stitch anyone up tonight."**

"Copy that," Captain Jordan replied. **"Alright, we stick to the plan. Bravo team will create a diversion on the west side. Alpha team, we're going in through the east. Turner, get those charges ready. We're going to need a quick entry."**

The Assault

The Green Berets split into two teams, moving with precision. Bravo team began their assault on the west side of the compound, drawing the attention of the guards and security forces. Explosions rocked the night as they unleashed a barrage of firepower, drawing the enemy's focus away from the real threat.

On the east side, the Alpha team advanced under the cover of the diversion. Captain Jordan led the way, and his senses heightened as they approached the outer wall. Staff Sergeant Turner moved ahead, carefully placing explosive charges at a weak point in the wall.

"**Charges set,**" Turner whispered, retreating to a safe distance. "**Blowing in three... two... one.**"

The explosion was controlled but powerful, blasting a hole in the wall large enough for the team to pass through. They moved quickly, slipping into the compound before the dust settled. Inside, the compound was a maze of corridors and fortified rooms, each more heavily guarded than the last.

"**Doc, take the point,**" Captain Jordan ordered. "**We must reach the inner sanctum before they know we're here.**"

Corporal Ramirez nodded, moving ahead with his rifle at the ready. The team advanced through the compound, engaging in brief but intense skirmishes with enemy guards. The Green Berets fought with lethal efficiency, their training and experience shining through as they neutralized each threat with minimal noise.

As they reached the inner courtyard, the intensity of the combat escalated. The Chinese guards were among the best in the world, and they fought fiercely to protect their leader. The courtyard became a battlefield, bullets whizzing through the air as both sides exchanged fire.

Sergeant Mike "Grizzly" Grant, a towering figure known for his strength and resilience, barked orders as he laid down suppressive fire. **"Keep pushing! We're almost there!"**

The Green Berets moved as a single unit, covering each other as they advanced toward the central building. They were met with a hail of bullets, but they pressed on, using every piece of cover available. The firefight was brutal, with both sides sustaining casualties.

"Turner, get that door open!" Captain Jordan shouted as they reached the entrance to the central building.

Staff Sergeant Turner moved forward, planting charges on the reinforced steel doors. The team took cover as the charges detonated, blasting the doors off their hinges. The Green Berets surged into the building, clearing rooms as they went.

The Inner Sanctum

The inner sanctum was the final stronghold, where only the most trusted guards were allowed. The Green Berets knew this was where they would face their most formidable challenge yet. The walls were lined with thick steel, and the corridors were narrow, designed to funnel intruders into kill zones.

Captain Jordan led the way, his weapon at the ready. **"Stay sharp. We're in the lion's den now."**

The team moved cautiously, every corner a potential ambush. Their breathing was loud in the confined space, but they remained focused. As they approached the final door, they heard the unmistakable sounds of frantic voices and movement inside.

"They know we're here," Corporal Ramirez muttered, gripping his rifle tighter.

Captain Jordan nodded. **"Good. Let's remind them why that's a bad thing."**

The team stacked up on either side of the door. Turner planted the last of his charges, and with a nod from Captain Jordan, the door was blown open. The Green Berets stormed into the room, weapons drawn, lasers trained on the occupants.

The Chinese leader stood at the room's far end, surrounded by his most loyal guards. His face was a mask of anger and fear as he realized the gravity of the situation. His guards opened fire, and the room erupted into chaos.

The Green Berets rushed, returning fire and systematically removing the guards. The room was filled with the loud sound of gunfire and the acrid smell of smoke. The guards fought fiercely, but they were no match for the Green Berets' skill and determination.

Within moments, the last of the guards fell, leaving the Chinese leader standing alone. He raised his hands slowly, his eyes wide with disbelief.

Captain Jordan stepped forward, his voice cold and commanding. **"It's over. You're coming with us."**

The Chinese leader sneered, but the fear in his eyes betrayed him. **"You'll never get out of here alive. My men will hunt you down."**

Captain Jordan met his gaze with unyielding resolve. **"They can try."**

Sergeant Grant moved in, binding the leader's hands with zip ties. The team quickly secured the room, ensuring there were no other threats. The mission had been brutal, but they had succeeded—they had captured the most powerful man in China.

"Extraction team, this is Alpha," Captain Jordan radioed. **"Target secured. Prepare for evac."**

The Extraction

The Green Berets moved swiftly, knowing they were still deep in enemy territory. The Chinese leader was kept under tight guard as they returned to the extraction point. The journey was fraught with danger, as they knew the compound's defensess would soon regroup and attempt to stop them.

As they reached the outer wall, the sounds of enemy reinforcements approaching grew louder. Captain Jordan turned to his team. **"We need to move, now! Turner, give us some cover!"**

Staff Sergeant Turner pulled out his last few charges, setting them along the wall as the team climbed through the breach. **"Fire in the hole!"** he shouted, detonating the charges just as the first wave of Chinese soldiers appeared.

The explosion created a cloud of smoke and debris, buying the Green Berets the time they needed to reach the extraction point. The sound of helicopter rotors filled the air as their ride appeared on the horizon.

"Move! Move!" Captain Jordan urged as the team sprinted toward the waiting helicopter.

They loaded the captive leader aboard the helicopter, securing him in place as the rest of the team climbed in. As the plane lifted off, they could see the chaos they had left behind—the compound in flames, the enemy forces scrambling in confusion.

Captain Jordan looked at the Chinese leader, now bound and gagged, sitting in the corner of the helicopter. **"Welcome to the endgame,"** he said, his voice grim. **"This is where we start taking back what's ours."**

The helicopter sped away, leaving the compound far behind. The Green Berets knew they had just dealt a crippling blow to their enemy. The mission had been the most challenging of their careers, but they had emerged victorious. The final puzzle piece had fallen into place, and now, the stage was set for the next phase of the war—a war they were determined to win.

Back in New America

James Alexander, along with the rest of the leadership, received the news with a mixture of relief and grim satisfaction. The missions had been successful, and the leaders of the occupying forces were now in New America's custody.

General Alexander addressed the nation in a televised broadcast. **"Today, we have struck a decisive blow against our enemies. The leaders who sought to oppress us are now in our hands. We will use this leverage to force them out of our lands once and for all. New America stands tall, united, and unbroken. The fight is not over, but victory is within our grasp."**

The nation cheered; their spirits lifted by the success of the daring operations. The tide had turned, and the liberation of the Americas was finally within reach.

Joint Intelligence

The Interrogation of the Chinese Leader

The journey back to New America was tense and exhausting, but the Green Berets had succeeded in their mission. The captured Chinese leader, a man who had orchestrated countless operations against the United States and its allies, now sat bound and silent in the back of the helicopter. His eyes darted around, taking in the grim faces of his captors, but he said nothing.

Upon arrival at the secret military base, the Chinese leader was immediately transferred into a high-security facility, where NSA and CIA operatives awaited his arrival. The facility, buried deep underground and shielded from any external surveillance, was designed for one purpose: to extract information from the most dangerous enemies of the state.

As the helicopter touched down on the pad, the Chinese leader was roughly pulled out and escorted by armed guards into the bowels of the facility. The Green Berets handed him off to a team of CIA operatives, who wasted no time in securing him in the interrogation room. The room was stark, with reinforced concrete walls, a single overhead light, and a metal table bolted to the floor. A steel chair awaited the prisoner.

The Arrival of the Interrogation Team

The door to the interrogation room swung open, and in walked a man with an air of authority. His name was Robert Sinclair, a seasoned CIA operative with decades of experience in counterintelligence. Following him was Dr. Emily Grant, an NSA psychologist known for breaking down even the most hardened minds.

Sinclair nodded to the guards, who shoved the Chinese leader into the chair and strapped him in. The leader glared at his captors but remained silent, his eyes betraying nothing.

"Good evening," Sinclair began, his voice smooth and controlled. He pulled out a chair on the opposite side of the table and sat down, placing a file folder in front of him. **"I'm Robert Sinclair, and this is Dr. Grant. We're here to have a little chat."**

The Chinese leader stared at Sinclair; his face expressionless. He was well-versed in psychological warfare and knew that showing any sign of weakness could be detrimental.

Sinclair leaned back in his chair, casually flipping open the folder. **"You've been quite the busy man,"** he said, glancing at the documents inside. **"Operations against American forces, cyberattacks on our infrastructure, alliances with some of the worst regimes in history. And now, here you are—our guest of honor."**

Still, the Chinese leader said nothing. Sinclair expected this; he knew the man before him was a master of silence. But Sinclair was patient, and he had time on his side.

Dr. Grant stepped forward, her calm and soothing voice filling the room. "You must be tired after such a long journey," she said. **"The body and mind can only endure so much before they need rest. We're prepared to offer you certain… comforts in exchange for your cooperation."**

The Chinese leader's lips curled into a slight smirk, the first real emotion he had shown. "**You think I will betray my country for comfort?**" he said in heavily accented English. "**You are fools.**"

Sinclair chuckled softly. "**Comfort? No. I wouldn't insult your intelligence by suggesting that. But information is valuable, and there are ways to make even the most resilient person reconsider their loyalty.**"

He leaned forward, his eyes locking onto the Chinese leader's. "**You see, we're not here to negotiate. We're here to get answers. You have the information we need, and we have the means to extract it.**"

The First Round of Questions

Sinclair placed a series of photographs on the table—images of critical Chinese military installations, high-ranking officials, and plans for operations intercepted by American intelligence. "Let's start with something simple," he said, tapping one of the photographs. "Tell us about this facility. We know it's significant, but we need details—personnel, defenses, anything you can give us."

The Chinese leader looked at the photograph but remained silent. His eyes shifted to Dr. Grant, who was watching him closely.

Dr. Grant leaned in, her voice soft but firm. **"You've been trained to resist interrogation, but everyone has a breaking point. The human mind is complex, and it's our job to find the cracks. We can do this the easy way, where you walk out of here alive and unharmed, or we can do this the hard way."**

The leader's eyes narrowed, and he spoke again, his tone icy. **"You think you can break me? I've endured worse than anything you can imagine. Your threats mean nothing."**

Sinclair smiled as if the leader's defiance was precisely what he had expected. **"That's what they all say at first. But they always talk in the end. The question is, how long it will take."**

He reached into the folder and pulled out a document, sliding it across the table. **"This is a list of Chinese operatives we've captured over the years. Some of them were in your position once. They resisted, just like you're doing now. But eventually, they broke. They gave us everything we needed—and more."**

The Chinese leader glanced at the document but quickly looked away. Sinclair could see the cracks forming but knew it would take more pressure to break through the wall.

Dr. Grant continued her tone, which became more insistent. **"Your country has abandoned you. You're here, in the hands of the people you've spent years trying to destroy, and no one is coming to save you. This is your reality now. The sooner you accept it, the easier this will be for you."**

The leader's jaw tightened, but he said nothing. Sinclair decided it was time to escalate.

Escalation

Sinclair stood up and walked around the table, his footsteps echoing in the small room. **"We have methods that can make even the strongest men talk. Sleep deprivation, sensory overload, psychological manipulation... the list goes on. You will talk, one way or another."**

He nodded to the guards, who immediately unstrapped the Chinese leader from the chair and hauled him to his feet. **"Take him to the holding cell,"** Sinclair ordered. **"We'll give him some time to think about his options."**

As the guards dragged the leader out of the room, Sinclair turned to Dr. Grant. **"Let's see how he holds up after a few days in isolation. No light, no sound, no human contact. That usually does the trick."**

Dr. Grant nodded. **"He's strong, but everyone has a limit. We'll monitor his psychological state and adjust our approach as needed."**

Isolation

The Chinese leader was thrown into a small, windowless cell, where the only sound was the faint hum of the ventilation system. The lights were always kept on, disorienting him and making it impossible to tell whether it was day or night. There was no bed, only a cold, hard floor. The food was minimal, just enough to keep him alive but not enough to sustain his strength.

Days he was passed in this state of sensory deprivation. The leader's mind began to fray as the isolation took its toll. The constant light made sleeping impossible, and the silence was maddening. He tried to keep his mind sharp by reciting mantras and focusing on training, but the strain was becoming too much to bear.

On the fourth day, the door to his cell opened, and Sinclair entered, accompanied by Dr. Grant. The leader squinted against the bright light, his eyes bloodshot and his face gaunt.

Sinclair crouched beside the Chinese leader, who was slumped against the wall, clearly weakened by the days of isolation. His once defiant expression had softened, replaced by a haunted look. The isolation had begun to wear him down, just as Sinclair had anticipated.

"**How are you holding up?**" Sinclair asked, his voice deceptively calm. He knew the leader was on the brink, and now was the time to press further.

The leader didn't respond immediately. His breathing was shallow, and his eyes flicked between Sinclair and Dr. Grant. The silence hung in the air, heavy with tension.

"**You've been through a lot these past few days,**" Sinclair continued, his tone almost sympathetic. "**But it doesn't have to be this way. You have the power to end this, to make it stop. All you must do is talk.**"

The leader finally spoke, his voice hoarse from lack of use. "**You're wasting your time,**" he rasped. "**I won't betray my people.**"

Sinclair sighed, standing up and walking a few steps away. "**You're a strong man, I'll give you that. But strength isn't always about enduring pain. Sometimes, it's about making the right choice, even when difficult.**"

Dr. Grant stepped forward, her voice gentle yet firm. "**You're alone here. Your government has disavowed you. They've moved on, focusing on their survival. Meanwhile, you're stuck in this cell, suffering for a cause already abandoned you.**"

The leader's eyes flashed with anger, but it was a fleeting emotion, quickly replaced by exhaustion. He knew the truth in their words, but admitting it was another matter entirely.

Sinclair leaned in closer, his voice dropping to a whisper. "**We don't want to break you. We want information. Give us what we need, and this ends. You get your life back. Maybe even a chance at something more.**"

The leader shook his head slowly, though his resolve was visibly weakening. **"I've endured worse than this… I can hold out longer."**

Dr. Grant crossed her arms, observing the man's deteriorating state. **"Perhaps. But at what cost? Your mind is already suffering. Prolonged isolation like this can cause irreversible damage—paranoia, hallucinations, and a complete breakdown of your cognitive abilities. Is that really what you want?"**

The leader looked down, his hands trembling slightly. The words sank in, each chipping away at the walls he had built around himself.

Sinclair decided it was time to apply a different kind of pressure. He signaled to one of the guards, who left the room briefly and returned with a small device. It was a tablet, and when the guard handed it to Sinclair, the screen lit up with a live video feed.

"This," Sinclair said, holding the tablet so the leader could see, **"is your family."**

The screen showed a well-guarded villa in the Chinese countryside, where the leader's wife and children lived under the protection of the state. They were unaware that the camera was capturing their every move and were going about their day as usual.

The leader's eyes widened in shock. He hadn't seen his family in months, not since the escalation of the conflict. Seeing them now, vulnerable and exposed, was a cruel reminder of what he stood to lose.

"You may be willing to endure this," Sinclair said, his voice cold now, **"but are you willing to put them through the same suffering? Because if you don't cooperate, we will ensure that they are affected by your choices."**

The leader's breathing became ragged, his hands clenching into fists. The mention of his family had struck a nerve, and Sinclair knew it. It was a line the leader had hoped they wouldn't cross, but there were no rules in this game.

"**I'll tell you what you want to know,**" the leader finally whispered, his voice breaking. "Just... leave them out of this. They're innocent."

Sinclair nodded, motioning for the guards to take the tablet away. "**You've made the right choice. Now, let's start from the beginning. Tell us about the Chinese government's military hierarchy structure, the key figures, and their plans.**"

The leader began to speak, his voice low and strained. He detailed the inner workings of the Chinese military, the locations of secret installations, the strategies they had developed to counter American forces, and the identities of operatives embedded in various countries.

Dr. Grant took notes, capturing every detail. Sinclair listened intently, occasionally asking for clarification or more information. The leader spoke slowly at first, but as the interrogation continued, the floodgates opened. He revealed more than they had hoped for—plans that had been in the works for years, alliances that threatened global stability, and weaknesses in the Chinese defensess that could be exploited.

Hours passed, and the information continued to flow. By the end, the Chinese leader was slumped over the table, utterly defeated. He had given up everything he knew and with it, any hope of returning to his former life.

Sinclair stood up, satisfied with the results. "**You've done the right thing,**" he said, though his voice had no warmth. "**Your cooperation will be noted.**"

As the guards escorted the broken man back to his cell, Dr. Grant turned to Sinclair. "**We've got everything we need. This could change the entire course of the war.**"

The Interrogation: The North Korean Leader

The room was cold and dimly lit; the only light source was a bulb hanging overhead. The walls were reinforced concrete, which didn't let sound escape. It was a place designed for one purpose: to break a man's will. In the center of the room, seated in a metal chair bolted to the floor, was the North Korean leader, Kim Yong-Jin. His hands were bound tightly to the armrests, and a heavy chain secured his feet to the chair's legs.

Across from him, two figures loomed in the shadows. One was a seasoned CIA operative, John Reynolds, known for his relentless and systematic approach to interrogation. The other was an NSA analyst, Karen Mitchell, an expert in psychological warfare and behavioral analysis. Together, they were assigned to extract the vital information New America needed to end the war.

Kim Yong-Jin had been in this room for hours, perhaps days. The steady clock ticking on the wall was the only sound that marked the passage of time. The relentless questioning had eroded his usually confident demeanor, but he maintained a defiant stare, refusing to show any sign of weakness.

Reynolds began the session, as always, with a deliberate, calm tone. **"Mr. Kim, you know why you're here. We've got a lot to talk about, and the sooner you start cooperating, the sooner we can resolve this. Tell us what we need to know, and this can all be over."**

Kim remained silent, his eyes narrowing as he studied his captors. His face was unreadable, but a bead of sweat trickled down his temple. He was used to giving orders and not being questioned, and the situation was unsettling.

Reynolds continued, unfazed by the silence. **"We know you're a key player in the operations against New America. We've already** taken down your allies. You're alone now, isolated. The sooner you accept that the easier this will be."

Mitchell leaned forward slightly; her voice soft yet piercing. "You may think you're strong enough to resist, Mr. Kim, but we know how to get what we want. Everyone has a breaking point. Yours is just a matter of time."

Kim finally spoke, his voice low and filled with contempt. "You Americans think you can control everything with your arrogance and power. But you've underestimated us. We will never bow to your demands."

Reynolds glanced at Mitchell, who nodded subtly. They had expected this defiance, a tactic they had encountered before. The real work was beginning.

"Arrogance?" Reynolds replied, his voice measured. "No, Mr. Kim, this isn't about arrogance. It's about survival—yours and ours. The sooner you understand that, the better it will be for you."

Mitchell leaned in closer, her eyes locking onto Kim's. "We're not asking for much. Just a few answers. Where are your strategic reserves? What are your next planned offensives? How deep does your alliance with China go? You give us this, and we can talk about your future. You refuse, and... well, let's say your future won't be very bright."

Kim's lips curled into a sneer. "You'll get nothing from me. I'll die before I betray my country."

Reynolds sighed as if disappointed. "That's where you're wrong, Mr. Kim. This isn't just about you. It's about the millions of people suffering because of your and your allies' decisions. Every second you resist, more lives are lost. That blood is on your hands."

The room fell silent again, the tension thick in the air. Kim's resolve was firm, but Reynolds and Mitchell had seen stronger men break. They knew it was only a matter of time.

"**Let's try a different approach,**" Mitchell suggested, her tone shifting to feigned empathy. "**You're a patriot, Mr. Kim. I understand that. You've devoted your life to your country. But think about what's happening right now. North Korea is in ruins, your people are suffering, and the world is turning against you. Do you want your legacy to be one of destruction and defeat?**"

Kim's eyes flickered for a moment, and Mitchell caught it. She pressed on, sensing an opening. "**You have the power to change that. Help us end this conflict, and we can ensure your people are spared further suffering. You could be remembered as the man who saved his nation from destruction.**"

Kim's expression hardened again, but there was a crack in his armor. Reynolds saw it, too, and decided to shift tactics. He leaned forward, his voice low and intense. "**Your people, Mr. Kim. The ones you swore to protect. They're the ones paying the price right now. We have intelligence on the ground, showing the devastation your country is facing. How long do you think they can hold out? How long before they turn on you, realizing the cause you've been fighting for is hopeless?**"

Kim's fists clenched on the armrests, the chains rattling slightly. The images that Reynolds and Mitchell painted were not far from the truth. He knew the situation in North Korea was dire but admitting that to these Americans felt like the ultimate betrayal.

Seeing his internal struggle, Mitchell went in for the final push. "**We're giving you a chance, Mr. Kim. A chance to save your people to secure a future for North Korea. But it's up to you. This can end with honor, or it can end in disaster. The choice is yours.**"

Kim's breath was coming faster now, the pressure bearing down on him. He knew they were right in some ways, but the thought of surrendering to his enemies was unbearable. He had to weigh his pride against the reality of his situation.

Reynolds stood, pacing slowly around the chair. **"We can make this easy, or we can make it hard. You can cooperate, and we'll do everything to ensure you're treated respectfully. Or you can resist, and... well, let's say the next phase of this interrogation won't be so pleasant."**

Kim's eyes followed Reynolds, his mind racing. He had been trained to resist and never give in, but the situation grew increasingly desperate. He was alone, his allies were captured or dead, and his country was on the brink of collapse. Was this fight worth continuing?

Mitchell leaned back in her chair, crossing her arms. **"Time's running out, Mr. Kim. You've held out longer than most; I'll give you that. But even the strongest men have limits. So, what's it going to be?"**

The room fell silent again, the tension thick enough to cut with a knife. Kim Yong-Jin's face was a mask of conflict, torn between his duty and the harsh reality he faced. Finally, he looked up, meeting Reynolds's gaze.

"What guarantees can you offer me?" Kim asked, his voice barely above a whisper, but there was a surrender note.

Reynolds and Mitchell exchanged glances, knowing they had him. The first step had been taken. Now, they could begin unraveling the information they needed.

"You cooperate fully," Reynolds said, **"and we'll ensure you're treated fairly. We'll work with you to secure a safe outcome for your people. But you need to give us something first."**

Kim hesitated, then nodded slowly. The decision was made, and North Korea's fate was sealed. He began to speak, revealing the secrets that would help New America turn the tide of the war, one confession at a time. The interrogation had broken him; now, there was no turning back.

The Interrogation: The Russian Leader

The room was silent, save for the distant hum of machinery that seemed to vibrate through the walls. The air was thick with tension, a mix of stale smoke and the faint metallic tang of blood. At the center of the room sat the Russian President, Viktor Ivanov, restrained in a heavy steel chair. Once commanding and full of authority, his face was now bruised and battered, but his eyes still burned with defiance.

Across from him stood two figures, one a hardened CIA operative, Agent Mark Dawson, and the other an NSA cyber-operations specialist, Dr. Elena Kozlov, who had been brought in for her deep understanding of Russian psychological warfare techniques. Dawson was the muscle who had spent years breaking men far tougher than Ivanov. Kozlov was the brain, a Russian-born American whose understanding of her former homeland's tactics made her invaluable in this operation.

Ivanov had been in this room for what felt like an eternity, the days blending into a haze of relentless questioning and psychological manipulation. He had been stripped of his dignity, but his resolve remained firm. The Russians were a proud people, and Ivanov was no exception. He knew what was at stake—his country, his legacy, and the future of his people.

Dawson began the session as always, his voice cold and clinical. **"Mr. Ivanov, you've been here for a while now. You know how this works. We can keep doing this the hard way, or you can make things easier for yourself. It's your choice."**

Ivanov stared back at him, his eyes filled with contempt. **"You Americans think you can bully the world into submission. But I suppose you might be wrong. Russia will never bow to your demands."**

Kozlov stepped forward, her voice softer but no less menacing. **"Mr. Ivanov, this isn't about submission. This is about survival. The** world has changed, and your regime is on the brink of collapse. Your allies are gone, your military is in disarray, and your people are suffering. Is this the legacy you want to leave behind?"

Ivanov's lips curled into a sneer. "**My people are strong. They have endured far worse than this, and they will endure again. You underestimate the Russian spirit.**"

Dawson leaned in, his voice a low growl. "**Spare me the patriotism, Viktor. This isn't about the Russian spirit. This is about you. You've lost, and you know it. The sooner you accept that the better off you'll be.**"

Ivanov's jaw tightened, but he remained silent. He was a man used to power, and the thought of losing it was unbearable. But the truth was becoming harder to ignore. His country was in shambles, his military was defeated, and his allies were captured or dead. The walls were closing in, and he knew it.

Kozlov continued, her tone almost sympathetic. "**Mr. Ivanov, I know what you're going through. I understand the pride of our people and the weight of responsibility you carry. But think about what's happening now. Your stubbornness is only prolonging the suffering of your people. Is that what you want?**"

Ivanov's gaze flickered, a hint of doubt creeping into his eyes. Kozlov had touched a nerve, and she knew it. She pressed on, sensing an opportunity.

"**You have the power to end this,**" she said softly. "**To save what's left of your country, to secure a future for your people. But it would be best if you worked with us. Help us bring this conflict to an end, and we'll do everything we can to ensure your people are spared further suffering.**"

Ivanov's fists clenched on the armrests, the chains rattling slightly. The images of his crumbling nation and the suffering of his people flashed through his mind. He had always prided himself on being a strong leader, but his strength was being tested in ways he had never imagined.

Dawson sensed the shift and moved in for the final blow. "**Your country is falling apart, Viktor. The longer you hold out, the worse it's going to get. You've already lost. Don't drag your people down with you. Give us what we need; you can still walk away from this with dignity.**"

Ivanov's eyes met Dawson's, and for the first time, there was a crack in his resolve. He was a man who had faced countless enemies, but now he was alone, facing the harsh reality of his situation. The defiance that had carried him through many battles was fading, replaced by a cold, creeping despair.

Kozlov leaned back, her arms crossed. "**This can end one of two ways, Mr. Ivanov. You can cooperate, and we'll ensure you're treated with the respect a man of your stature deserves. Or you can continue to resist, and we'll take other measures to get what we need. The choice is yours.**"

The room fell silent, the tension thick enough to cut with a knife. Ivanov's face was a mask of inner turmoil, his mind racing as he weighed his options. He had been taught never to surrender or fight to the bitter end, but the situation grew increasingly desperate.

Finally, Ivanov spoke, his voice strained but resigned. "**What do you want to know?**"

Dawson and Kozlov exchanged a glance, knowing they had won. The Russian leader had finally broken, and now, they could begin to extract the information they needed to cripple the last remnants of the enemy forces.

"Start with your military's strategic reserves," Dawson said, his tone firm but not unkind. **"Where are they located? What's their status?"**

Ivanov hesitated, then spoke, revealing the secrets to help New America end the war. Each word felt like a betrayal, but he knew no other choice. The interrogation had shattered his defenses, and now, all that was left was to salvage what little he could of his legacy.

As the hours passed, Ivanov divulged everything he knew—military positions, strategic plans, and the weaknesses of his former allies. With each revelation, the once-mighty leader seemed to shrink, the weight of his defeat pressing down on him.

Finally, when there was nothing left to give, Ivanov slumped in his chair, his energy spent. Dawson and Kozlov knew they had extracted every piece of valuable information. The war was nearing its end, and with it, Viktor Ivanov's reign.

As they prepared to leave, Kozlov paused by the door, turning back to the broken man who had once ruled with an iron fist. **"You did the right thing, Viktor. History will remember you for this."**

Ivanov didn't respond, his eyes fixed on a distant point on the wall. The man who had once commanded the fear and respect of millions was now just another casualty of a war that had claimed too many lives. The interrogation was over, but the consequences of his decisions would echo through history.

The Enemy Respond

NEW AMERICAN COMMAND CENTER

The large, fortified command center is bustling with activity. Screens flicker with live feeds, data streams, and maps tracking global movements. The NEW AMERICA NATIONAL COMMITTEE, composed of military leaders, intelligence officials, and civilian authorities, sits around a large table, their faces etched with concern.

As the leaders of New America watched the screens before them, the world outside their walls teetered on the brink of chaos. The daring kidnappings of the Chinese, Russian, and North Korean leaders had ignited a firestorm of retaliation.

CHINESE MILITARY HEADQUARTERS - BEIJING

Field Commander WANG stands rigidly before his generals, eyes locked on a screen displaying satellite images of New America. **"Mobilize the troops immediately. I want every division on high alert and ready to advance on New America's borders. Initiate cyber operations—bring down their power grids, disrupt their communications, and ensure they cannot respond."**

In Beijing, the General Wang, wasted no time. With their leader in the hands of New America, the Chinese military was ordered to prepare for an invasion. But before the boots could hit the ground, they aimed to cripple New America from within.

NEW AMERICAN COMMAND CENTER

The lights flicker momentarily, causing a brief pause in the room. COMMANDER JONES, the head of cyber defenses, quickly assesses the situation. **"General Carter, China has launched a massive cyber-attack. We're seeing disruptions in our power grids and communications networks."**

GENERAL CARTER nods grimly, issuing commands with a steady hand.

"**Engage our cyber defensess. I want every available resource allocated to countering this attack. We can't afford to lose control now.**" Within moments, New America's defensess scrambled to respond to the digital assault, battling to keep the lights on and the lines of communication open.

RUSSIAN KREMLIN WAR ROOM - MOSCOW

The military commanders came together to address the situation.

Comrade Ivanov, the fleet admiral, commanded, "**Activate our nuclear submarines. I want them positioned near New America's coastline, ready to strike. And send in the Spetsnaz—they must retrieve our leader at all costs.**"

The spectre of nuclear war loomed as Russian submarines crept closer to New America. Meanwhile, elite Spetsnaz units were dispatched with one mission: retrieve their leader, no matter the cost.

NEW AMERICAN COMMAND CENTER

ADMIRAL BEASLEY, responsible for naval operations, looks at the shifting positions on the map with mounting concern. The Russian navy had dispatched almost their entire fleet to reposition themselves in American waters.

Intelligence officers directed a communication from the Russian Fleet commander, "Admiral, Russian nuclear submarines are advancing on our coast. They're not making any attempts to hide their movements. We need to prepare for the worst."

GENERAL CARTER exchanges a tense look at ALEXANDER, the head of the New America Committee. "**Mr. Chairman let's not provoke them just yet. Keep our subs in defensive positions and increase our surveillance. We need to know their every move.**"

The New America Committee knew the gravity of the situation. A single misstep could trigger a nuclear confrontation, ending the fragile new state before it had fully taken root.

The command center is a hive of focused activity. Monitors display real-time intelligence, with various feeds tracking the movements of enemy forces. As the NATIONAL COMMITTEE sits around a large table, their expressions are a mix of determination and readiness. GENERAL CARTER stands at the head, looking over the room. From the moment the plan was set in motion, New America knew the enemy would not take the kidnappings lightly. They had anticipated the response—every move, every countermove. One thing was sure: no heavy artillery or nuclear weapons would be launched in the bid to free their leaders.

The committee stands gazing at a digital map. INTELLIGENCE CHIEF HANSON steps forward, his voice calm and measured. **"We've analysed the enemy's likely responses. While they may rattle their sabres and mobilize their forces, they won't risk nuclear war or heavy artillery strikes. They know they would be crossing a line even if they can't afford it."**

Chairman Alexander nods, his eyes narrowing as he considers the implications. **"They'll try to retrieve their leaders covertly special forces, cyber warfare, psychological operations. We need to be prepared for infiltration attempts and sabotage."**

General Carter nodded, "Agreed. We've fortified our positions and heightened security across all sensitive sites. Our forces are on high alert, and we've deployed countermeasures to prevent surprise attacks."

New America's leadership had taken every precaution. They knew their enemies would attempt to retrieve their leaders by any means necessary—but they were ready.

RUSSIAN KREMLIN WAR ROOM - MOSCOW

IVANOV clenches his fists as he listens to reports from his generals. One exclaimed, **"Sir, they've fortified their positions. A direct assault with heavy artillery could provoke a full-scale war that none of us would walk away from."**

The command center is a maze of glowing monitors and steady murmurs, the heartbeat of New America's military operations. A sense of urgency pervades the room, though every movement is deliberate and precise. Standing stern and composed, GENERAL CARTER oversees the situation.

The New American Command Center buzzed with activity as the night deepened. General Carter stood at the helm, surveying the room as reports came in. Commander Jones approached, delivering the latest news: another failed attempt by Spetsnaz units to infiltrate their defensess. General Carter barely reacted, his calm demeanor reflecting the confidence that had been building with each thwarted attack. "That's the third attempt this week," Jones noted, frustration tinging his voice. "They're getting desperate." Carter allowed himself a slight smile, knowing that their defensess had held firm. He instructed the communications officer to stay vigilant, ensuring every contingency plan was airtight.

The atmosphere in the intelligence briefing room the next day was equally intense. Intelligence Chief Hanson briefed the assembled officers on the latest enemy tactics, detailing how Chinese operatives had been neutralized before reaching their target. President Alexander listened intently, acknowledging the growing desperation of their adversaries. General Carter reinforced their strategy, stating confidently that no one would breach their security. The leadership was resolute, determined to maintain their grip on the situation and deny the enemy any chance of success.

Meanwhile, in the heart of occupied America, the resistance fighters were engaged in a different battle. In a dimly lit safehouse, resistance leaders unpacked crates of smuggled supplies—food, ammunition, and weapons—relief washing over them as they realized they were no longer on the brink of depletion. A young fighter tested a newly acquired rifle, his resolve hardening with the feel of the weapon in his hands. The resistance leader emphasized the importance of their mission, knowing that each successful operation would keep their fight alive and strengthen their connection to New America.

Deep underground, the resistance's covert operations were in full swing. A team of fighters navigated a narrow tunnel, carefully transporting crates to hidden caches spread throughout the network. They worked quickly and silently, their movements precise and practiced. Once the supplies were distributed, they vanished into the darkness, leaving no trace of their presence.

Back at the New American Command Center, General Carter received a secure communication confirming the success of the latest supply run. He shared the news with President Alexander, who allowed a moment of satisfaction to cross his face. The successful resupply of the resistance meant that the fight would continue, and New America was fulfilling its promise to support those still under occupation. General Carter affirmed their commitment, ensuring the resistance would never feel abandoned. President Alexander, burdened by their ongoing struggle, resolved to keep the lifeline open, knowing that their ultimate victory depended on it.

At the NSA Operations Center, a young cryptologist named Jennifer Collins is alerted to an unusual, encrypted transmission from a Russian spy network. The complex signal, which involves Chinese and North Korean ciphers, indicates something significant. Jennifer and her team work tirelessly to decode the message, piecing together fragments that reveal a coordinated plan to recover the captured Russian, Chinese, and North Korean leaders. The information, once decoded, is quickly escalated to the Director of the NSA, who recognizes the urgency of the situation. The enemy's rescue operation is set to take place within the next 72 hours, leaving little time for New America to respond.

In a secure briefing, the Director of the NSA informs President James Alexander and the top military leaders, including the newly appointed General of the Army. They discuss the decoded message's implications and formulate a plan not only to defend against the rescue attempt but to use it as an opportunity to cripple the enemy's leadership further. A covert meeting in a secure bunker brings together military strategists and intelligence officers, who craft a counter-trap. The plan involves using the captured enemy leaders as bait, luring the enemy forces into a carefully orchestrated ambush. Special Forces units, including Navy SEALs, Army Rangers, and Green Berets, are briefed on their roles in the operation to capture or eliminate the enemy operatives involved in the rescue attempt.

Meanwhile, the Russian, Chinese, and North Korean forces moved into position, unaware that their plan had been compromised. Top military officials from each nation coordinated their strategy, confident in the success of their mission. The enemy operatives deployed with stealth and precision, infiltrating New American territory with minimal resistance. Their initial success bolstered their confidence, but subtle clues, such as overly easy access and a lack of significant defensess, hinted at the trap they were walking into.

The trap is sprung just as the enemy forces believe they are about to achieve their objective.

Having laid in wait, the New American forces launch a coordinated and overwhelming attack. The enemy operatives, caught off-guard, face intense and sudden resistance. In the ensuing close-quarters combat, the highly skilled Russian and Chinese forces are unprepared for the ferocity and precision of the New American response. The battle is fierce, with detailed descriptions of firefights, tactical maneuvers, and the chaos of war. Several enemy leaders are captured, while others are eliminated in the firefight. The SEALs, Rangers, and Green Berets move ruthlessly, ensuring no loose ends remain. As the enemy forces close in, the 82nd Airborne Division, who have been training in an undisclosed location for a mission of this magnitude, receive their orders. With their unparalleled combat readiness and expertise in airborne operations, they are called upon to eliminate the threat and execute the counter-trap. The division swiftly mobilizes, their training paying off as they prepare for immediate deployment.

The 82nd Airborne, known for their rapid response capabilities, parachute into strategically selected locations under the cover of night, surrounding the enemy operatives. Their precision and discipline ensure that the enemy has no chance to regroup or escape. As the operation unfolds, the 82nd Airborne moves with lethal efficiency, engaging the enemy forces in coordinated assaults that leave no room for error.

The 82nd Airborne's sudden appearance utterly overwhelmed the enemy. The division's presence decisively turned the tide of the battle in favor of New America. The remaining enemy operatives were either captured or neutralized, effectively dismantling the rescue operation.

With the threat eliminated, the 82nd Airborne secures the area, ensuring that any potential reinforcements or secondary plans by the enemy are thwarted. The mission's success is a testament to its training and the meticulous planning by New America's leadership. As the dust settles, the division prepares for its next assignment, knowing that its role in this operation is critical to maintaining the security and stability of the new nation.

As the enemy forces close in, the 82nd Airborne Division, which has been training in an undisclosed location for a mission of this magnitude, receives its orders. With its unparalleled combat readiness and expertise in airborne operations, the division is called upon to eliminate the threat and execute the counter-trap. The division swiftly mobilizes, its training paying off as it prepares for immediate deployment.

The 82nd Airborne, known for their rapid response capabilities, parachute into strategically selected locations under the cover of night, surrounding the enemy operatives. Their precision and discipline ensure that the enemy has no chance to regroup or escape. As the operation unfolds, the 82nd Airborne moves with lethal efficiency, engaging the enemy forces in coordinated assaults that leave no room for error.

The enemy, already caught off-guard by the initial New American response, is now completely overwhelmed by the sudden appearance of the 82nd Airborne. The division's presence turns the tide of the battle decisively in favor of New America. The remaining enemy operatives are either captured or neutralized, effectively dismantling the rescue operation and solidifying New America's dominance in this confrontation.

With the threat eliminated, the 82nd Airborne secures the area, ensuring that any potential reinforcements or secondary plans by the enemy are thwarted. The mission's success is a testament to its training and the meticulous planning by New America's leadership. As the dust settles, the division prepares for its next assignment, knowing that its role in this operation is critical to maintaining the security and stability of the new nation.

In the early hours of dawn, intelligence reports confirmed that a group of elite Russian soldiers, remnants of the failed rescue operation, had taken refuge in a secluded farmhouse deep within enemy-occupied territory. The soldiers, known for their exceptional training and combat experience, posed a significant threat if allowed to regroup or escape. The 82nd Airborne Division, specifically selected for this mission due to its rigorous training and combat readiness, was tasked with neutralizing this enemy force.

Colonel Mark Thompson, a highly respected and heroic officer within the 82nd Airborne, was assigned to lead the operation. Understanding the gravity of the situation and the importance of precise communication, Colonel Thompson meticulously planned the assault, ensuring that his 15-man team was fully briefed and prepared for the high-stakes engagement.

Pre-Operation Briefing:

Before the operation commenced, Colonel Thompson gathered his team for a final briefing. The atmosphere was tense but focused as each soldier understood the dangers they were about to face. Colonel Thompson's clear and direct communication emphasized the importance of stealth, coordination, and discipline.

"We have a group of well-trained Russian soldiers holed up in that farmhouse," Colonel Thompson began, his voice steady but authoritative. **"These aren't just any soldiers—they're elite and desperate. Desperation makes them dangerous. Our mission is to take them out quickly and efficiently. We can't afford any mistakes."**

He then detailed the plan, breaking down the operation into distinct phases. Each soldier was assigned a specific role, with contingencies for every possible scenario. Colonel Thompson clarified that communication would be the key to their success. He emphasized the importance of maintaining radio silence until the last possible moment to avoid alerting the enemy to their presence.

"Once we're in position, I want absolute silence until I give the go," Thompson instructed. **"If anything changes, if anyone sees something that needs addressing, you signal your team lead. Team leads, you report directly to me. We move as one unit, strike as one unit, and finish this as one unit."**

Movement into Position:

The team moved under the cover of darkness, advancing toward the farmhouse with deliberate and practiced precision. Colonel Thompson maintained a close watch over his men, using hand signals to direct their movements as they approached the target. Each soldier understood their position, ensuring they were in place to surround the farmhouse from all angles.

As they neared their objective, Colonel Thompson communicated with his team leads using pre-arranged signals. He double-checked their positions, ensuring that everyone was ready for the assault. The final communication before the attack was a simple but powerful gesture: a clenched fist followed by a pointed finger toward the farmhouse. It was the signal to prepare for engagement.

Initiating the Assault:

When the team was in position, Colonel Thompson initiated the attack with a single, decisive command over the radio: **"Execute."**

In an instant, the silence of the early morning was shattered by the controlled chaos of the assault. The team moved in with lethal precision, simultaneously breaching the farmhouse from multiple entry points. Colonel Thompson monitored the operation closely, communicating with his team leads to ensure that each plan element was executed flawlessly.

"Breach, breach, breach!" Thompson ordered, his voice calm yet commanding over the radio. The sound of doors being forced open and the rapid exchange of gunfire echoed through the radio as each team member reported their progress.

"First floor clear," one team lead reported.

"Second floor, room by room," Thompson responded, directing the team to proceed cautiously, knowing that the Russian soldiers would likely make a final stand.

Engagement and Outcome:

The communication during the engagement was crisp and efficient. Colonel Thompson's leadership ensured that his men maintained their composure, even as they encountered fierce resistance from the entrenched Russian soldiers. Despite the intense firefight, the team's discipline and adherence to their training allowed them to methodically clear the farmhouse, neutralizing the enemy one room at a time.

"**Top floor secure**," another team lead reported, the relief evident in his voice.

"**Confirm all clear**," Thompson ordered, refusing to relax until he was confident the mission was complete.

After a tense few moments, the final confirmation came through. "**All clear, Colonel. Mission accomplished.**"

Colonel Thompson took a moment to acknowledge the operation's success, his voice filled with pride and exhaustion. "**Well done, men. Regroup and prepare for extraction.**"

Post-Operation Debrief:

Following the successful assault, Colonel Thompson conducted a debrief with his team. The focus was on what had gone well and where improvements could be made for future operations. He commended his men for their professionalism and effective communication, highlighting how their ability to maintain clear and concise communication under pressure was critical to the mission's success.

"**Today, you showed what it means to be part of the 82nd Airborne**," Colonel Thompson said, his voice carrying the weight of experience and respect. "**We faced a well-trained enemy in a fortified position, and we came out on top because we stuck to our training and communicated effectively. That's what makes us the best.**"

The operation against the elite Russian soldiers was a decisive victory, not just in terms of tactical success but also in showcasing the importance of communication in high-risk military engagements. Colonel Thompson's leadership and the team's ability to execute the plan with precision were a testament to the effectiveness of the 82nd Airborne Division's training and the crucial role of clear, strategic communication in the field.

Diplomatic Showdown: The First Meeting with the Enemy

Introduction

The stakes could not have been higher as representatives from the New American government and military prepared for their first face-to-face meeting with enemy forces—Russian, Chinese, and North Korean officials. The objective was clear: state New America's demands for the evacuation of the occupied states in exchange for the release of the captured enemy leaders. This moment would not only set the tone for negotiations but could also determine the future course of the conflict. The tension was palpable as both sides understood that this meeting was more than just a diplomatic engagement; it was a battle of wills where any sign of weakness could tip the scales toward war.

Setting the Stage

The location chosen for the meeting was deliberately neutral—a nondescript building on the outskirts of what was once American territory but now lay within the zone controlled by the invading forces. Security was paramount, with elite units from both sides ensuring the area was secure. The environment was deliberately sparse, with a long, rectangular table dominating the center of the room. On one side sat the New American delegation, led by the General of the Army and senior government officials. On the other side, the enemy representatives, each projecting a cold confidence, settled into their seats.

As the delegates entered the room, the atmosphere was charged with an unspoken tension. The room reflected the seriousness of the occasion—plain, almost sterile, with only the flags of the involved nations serving as a reminder of the identities at play. Although distant, the eyes of the world were figuratively fixed on this room, awaiting the outcome that could lead to a fragile peace or further descent into chaos.

Opening Statements

The general of the Army, representing New America, initiated the meeting with an opening statement that was as firm as it was measured. **"We are here today because the people of New America believe in the possibility of peace, but not at the expense of our sovereignty and freedom. The occupation of our states is unacceptable, and we are prepared to take whatever actions are necessary to ensure the liberation of our lands."**

The enemy delegation listened intently, their expressions betraying little emotion. They were seasoned diplomats and military leaders, well-versed in negotiating under pressure. The Russian envoy, a veteran general with decades of experience, responded first. His voice was deep and authoritative as he articulated his nation's stance. **"We understand the demands of New America, but you must realize that the actions of your former government brought about the current situation. We are not here to discuss surrender but rather to negotiate favorable terms to all parties involved."**

This exchange set the tone for the meeting—a delicate dance of words where each side sought to assert its position without revealing too much. The New American delegation was acutely aware that their demands would be met with resistance, but they also knew that the captured leaders were valuable bargaining chips. The challenge was to leverage this advantage without provoking an escalation.

Negotiation Tactics

The negotiations quickly moved into the tactical phase, where each side began to lay out its terms. New America's demands were straightforward: the immediate and unconditional evacuation of the thirty occupied states, coupled with a guarantee of non-aggression in the future. In return, the captured Russian, Chinese, and North Korean leaders would be released unharmed. The request was explicit—New America would not settle for anything less than the complete withdrawal of enemy forces.

To reinforce their position, the New American delegation presented evidence of the captured leaders' well-being, showing they were treated according to international standards. This was a calculated move designed to remind the enemy that while their leaders were in custody, they could still be returned safely—if the demands were met.

The Chinese envoy, a sharp and calculating diplomat, responded with a counterproposal. He acknowledged the importance of the captured leaders but insisted that the withdrawal could only occur in stages, with each phase contingent upon the safe return of their leaders. This tactic was intended to buy time, allowing the occupying forces to regroup and potentially fortify their positions.

General of the Army rejected this proposal outright, understanding the dangers of a piecemeal approach. "A staged withdrawal is not acceptable. Our people have suffered enough under your occupation. The only path forward is a complete and immediate evacuation. We are prepared to ensure the safe return of your leaders, but this is non-negotiable."

The Russian and North Korean envoys, recognizing the resolve in the New American stance, attempted to shift the focus to other issues, such as potential economic reparations or the establishment of demilitarized zones. However, the New American delegation remained unwavering, refusing to be drawn into discussions that would dilute the primary objective—regaining complete control of the occupied states.

Escalation and Tensions

As the meeting progressed, the atmosphere grew increasingly tense. The enemy representatives began to exhibit frustration, their initial confidence giving way to concern. They realized New America was not merely posturing but was genuinely prepared to escalate the situation if their demands were unmet.

The turning point came when the North Korean envoy, known for his fiery rhetoric, issued a thinly veiled threat. **"You must understand that any harm to our leaders will be met with severe consequences. We will not hesitate to respond with full military force if necessary."**

General of the Army, unshaken by the threat, responded with a calm but stern warning. **"Let me be clear—any attempt to retaliate will be met with overwhelming force. The safety of your leaders is in your hands. Meet our demands, and they will be returned safely. Refuse, and you risk the lives of your leaders, soldiers, and citizens."**

This exchange underscored the high stakes of the negotiation. Both sides were aware that a misstep could lead to a catastrophic escalation. The room was thick with tension as each delegate weighed their options, knowing that the decisions made in this room could alter the course of history.

Strategic Leverage

Recognizing that the direct approach led to a stalemate, the New American delegation employed a different strategy. They introduced a series of strategic incentives designed to appeal to the self-interest of the enemy nations. These included economic partnerships, access to New American resources, and the potential for future diplomatic engagement, all contingent upon the complete withdrawal from the occupied states.

Sensing an opportunity, the Chinese envoy leaned in and asked for specifics regarding the economic partnerships. This shift in focus was precisely what the New American delegation hoped—a chance to introduce a new dynamic into the negotiations that could lead to a breakthrough.

General of the Army outlined a series of potential agreements that could benefit the enemy nations economically, emphasizing that these opportunities would only be available if the occupation ended. **"You have much to gain from a peaceful resolution,"** he explained. **"The resources and partnerships we offer could greatly benefit your nations, but only if we can reach an agreement today."**

The enemy envoys, particularly the Chinese and Russian representatives, appeared to consider this proposal seriously. They understood the economic benefits at stake, and for the first time in the meeting, there was a glimmer of hope that a resolution could be within reach.

The Turning Point

The meeting reached its critical juncture when the New American delegation presented a final offer: a detailed plan for the evacuation of the occupied states, complete with timelines and guarantees for the safe return of the captured leaders. The plan was structured to ensure that both sides would honor their commitments, with international observers overseeing the process to prevent any breaches of the agreement.

After consulting briefly with his counterparts, the Russian envoy finally spoke: **"This proposal is... reasonable. We will require assurances that the evacuation will proceed smoothly and that our leaders will be returned without delay."**

General of the Army responded decisively. **"You have our word, backed by international law and the eyes of the world. The choice is yours—accept this agreement and ensure the safe return of your leaders or refuse and face the consequences."**

Realizing they had no other options, the enemy envoys reluctantly agreed to the terms. The first step toward de-escalation had been taken, but the road ahead would be challenging. Both sides knew that trust was fragile, and that any misstep could reignite the conflict.

The first meeting between New America and the enemy forces was a high-stakes encounter that tested both sides' resolve, strategy, and diplomacy. New America's demands for the evacuation of the occupied states were met with resistance, but a tentative agreement was reached through a combination of firm resolve and strategic incentives.

This meeting marked the beginning of a potential de-escalation of the conflict. Still, it also highlighted the deep mistrust and lingering tensions that must be addressed in future negotiations. The success of this initial meeting depended mainly on the skillful communication and strategic leverage employed by the New American delegation, led by the General of the Army. Their ability to balance firmness with diplomacy set the stage for a possible resolution to the conflict. Still, the outcome would ultimately depend on the willingness of both sides to honor their commitments and pursue a path to peace.

Setting the Stage: Troops on Both Sides of the Fence

The New World Committee wasted no time in setting up a line of defenses that would stretch across the entirety of the border between New America and the occupied states. This line, dubbed "the Fence," was fortified with military installations, heavily armed troops, and advanced surveillance technology. The Fence was more than just a physical barrier—it symbolized the division that had torn the country apart.

On the New American side, troops were stationed strategically, ready to repel any enemy incursion. These battle-hardened soldiers had trained rigorously for the war they knew was coming. Their orders were clear: hold the line at all costs and be prepared to launch a counteroffensive when the time came.

The enemy forces, aware of the Committee's intentions, mirrored these preparations on their side of the Fence. They established their fortifications, deploying elite units trained in guerrilla warfare, cyber-attacks, and psychological operations. The stage was set for a conflict that would pit some of the world's most formidable military forces against each other in a battle for control over the United States.

Naval Blockades and the Threat of Total Destruction

While the Fence was the focal point for ground operations, the New World Committee understood that sea control would be crucial in this war. Under Admiral Jim Beasley's command, the Navy established a naval blockade around the occupied states. The goal was simple: prevent enemy reinforcements or supplies from reaching their shores and destroy enemy ships that dared to challenge the blockade.

The Navy's presence was overwhelming, with aircraft carriers, destroyers, and submarines patrolling the waters around the clock. These ships were armed with the latest in missile technology and could deliver devastating strikes against enemy vessels. The message to the enemy was clear: any attempt to breach the naval blockade would be met with swift destruction.

Tensions on the high seas escalated rapidly. The enemy navies, though outnumbered, were not to be underestimated. They began to probe the blockade, sending submarines to test the defensess and deploying aircraft to gather intelligence. Skirmishes broke out frequently, with both sides suffering losses. However, the New

American Navy's superior firepower ensured that the enemy never gained the upper hand.

The horror of the naval warfare was palpable. Ships that were once symbols of national pride were now reduced to burning wrecks, and their crews were lost to the ocean's cold depths. Survivors who managed to escape the sinking vessels were left to drift in the water, their fates uncertain as they awaited rescue or death.

The War on the Ground: A Symphony of Violence

The war on the ground intensified as the naval blockade tightened its grip on the enemy's supply lines. The New World Committee, having completed their preparations, launched a series of coordinated assaults across the Fence. These attacks were designed to weaken the enemy's defensess and reclaim strategic positions within the occupied states.

The fighting was fierce and unrelenting. Entire towns and cities became battlegrounds, with buildings reduced to rubble and streets littered with the bodies of soldiers and civilians alike. The enemy, well-entrenched and determined to hold their ground, fought back with a ferocity that surprised even the most seasoned New American troops.

The New American forces, however, were not without their brutal tactics. In their quest to reclaim their homeland, they employed methods that blurred the lines between conventional warfare and outright atrocities. Villages suspected of harbouring enemy soldiers were bombed into oblivion, and their inhabitants were left to burn in the ensuing fires. Enemy prisoners were subjected to harsh interrogations, with many never making it out of the camps alive.

As the war dragged on, the psychological toll on both sides became evident. Soldiers who had once fought with a sense of duty and honor now found themselves descending into madness, driven by the horrors they had witnessed and perpetrated. Reports of war crimes began to surface, with both New American and enemy forces accused of committing unspeakable acts in the heat of battle.

The cities of the occupied states became hellscapes, with entire neighbourhoods turned into war zones. Civilians who had once lived ordinary lives now found themselves trapped in the crossfire, their homes and livelihoods destroyed. The war had no mercy for anyone, soldier or civilian, and the death toll rose with each passing day.

Chemical Warfare: The Ultimate Horror

As the ground war escalated, both sides began to resort to increasingly desperate measures. The New World Committee, recognizing the strategic importance of some enemy-held regions, authorized the use of chemical weapons to flush out entrenched enemy forces. The decision was controversial, but the Committee argued that it was a necessary evil to end the war quickly.

The first use of chemical weapons came during the siege of a key city in the Midwest. New American forces, unable to breach the enemy's defensess through conventional means, launched a series of chemical attacks that blanketed the city in a toxic cloud. The effects were immediate and devastating. Enemy soldiers, caught without adequate protection, succumbed to the gas in horrific ways—gasping for breath, their skin blistering, and their eyes burning.

But it wasn't just the enemy who suffered. Civilians who had been unable to evacuate the city were also caught in the chemical attacks. The images that emerged from the aftermath were haunting streets filled with the bodies of men, women, and children who had died in agony. The once-thriving city was now a ghost town, its buildings still standing, but its population decimated.

The enemy, in retaliation, launched their chemical attacks on New American positions. The horrors of chemical warfare spread across the front lines, with soldiers on both sides donning gas masks as they fought in landscapes that resembled the battlefields of World War I. The air was thick with the smell of death, and the lingering clouds of toxic gas now obscured the once-clear skies.

The use of chemical weapons marked a turning point in the war. The New World Committee, once determined to liberate the occupied states, now found themselves trapped in a cycle of escalating violence that threatened to consume everything in its path. The moral high ground they once claimed was lost, replaced by a growing despair and hopelessness.

The Human Cost

As the war dragged on, the human cost became impossible to ignore. Millions of lives were lost, and those who survived were forever scarred by the experiences they had endured. The soldiers who fought on both sides returned home as broken men, haunted by the memories of the atrocities they had witnessed and committed.

Civilians, too, bore the brunt of the war's horrors. The occupied states, once vibrant and thriving, were now wastelands, with entire communities wiped out by the fighting. Those who had managed to escape the war zones were left to wander as refugees, their homes destroyed and their futures uncertain.

The psychological impact of the war was. Once hailed as liberators, the New American troops were now viewed with suspicion and fear by the people they had fought to save. The enemy forces, too, were shattered by the conflict, their morale crushed by the relentless onslaught of the New American military.

The New World Committee, having achieved its objective of reclaiming the occupied states, now faced the daunting task of rebuilding a nation torn apart by war. But the victory, if it could be called that, came at a terrible price. The country was divided, its people traumatized, and its future uncertain.

The war between New America and the occupying forces was a conflict of unprecedented brutality and horror. The New World Committee, in their quest to reclaim the lost territories, unleashed a wave of violence that left no one untouched. The war was marked by acts of unimaginable cruelty, with both sides resorting to increasingly desperate measures in their bid for victory.

Ultimately, the New World Committee succeeded in its mission, but the cost was staggering. The country they had fought to save was now a shadow of its former self, its people scarred by the horrors of war. The victory was hollow, and whether it was worth the price would haunt the nation for years.

The war served as a grim reminder of the destructive power of human conflict and the lengths to which people will go when faced with an existential threat. It was a war that should never have happened, but once it did, it unleashed a darkness that could never be fully extinguished. The legacy of the New World Committee's war would be felt for generations, a testament to the horrors of a divided nation and the price of reclaiming lost glory.

The Battle of the Ravine: A Grim Turn of Fate

Introduction

The ravine was deep, jagged, and shadowed by towering cliffs, a natural deathtrap that could easily be mistaken for a sanctuary by those desperate to seek refuge there. The Russian forces, confident in their relentless pursuit of the retreating Americans, had unknowingly driven them straight into what seemed to be an inescapable end. They believed the Americans were cornered, with no way out, and that victory was imminent. But they were wrong—wrong.

The American forces had planned this moment down to the smallest detail. The Russians didn't know they were being lured into a carefully laid trap, one that would see them surrounded by a force far more significant than they had ever imagined. As the Russian soldiers advanced into the ravine, the ground beneath them was about to turn into the stage for one of the war's most brutal and decisive battles.

The Russians' Pursuit

The Russian commander, General Mikhail Petrov, surveyed the terrain from a ridge, his binoculars trained on the fleeing American troops below. The Americans were moving fast, but they needed to be faster. Petrov could sense the desperation in their retreat, the way they scrambled over rocks and stumbled through the uneven terrain.

"They're cornered," Petrov said, lowering his binoculars. He turned to his second-in-command, Colonel Ivanov. **"They have nowhere to go. Once they hit that ravine, they're done for."**

Ivanov nodded, a wicked grin spreading across his face. **"We'll crush them here, General. This will be the end of the American resistance in this sector."**

Petrov's troops shared his confidence, pushing forward with renewed vigour. The Americans had been a thorn in their side for far too long, and now, finally, they had them where they wanted them.

The ravine was a perfect trap—or so they thought. The Russians believed they had outmaneuvered the Americans, forcing them into a cul-de-sac from which there was no escape. But in their eagerness to claim victory, they failed to notice the subtle signs of a more significant force lying in wait.

The Americans' Plan

Colonel Blake Dill, the American commander, watched as the last of his men disappeared into the narrow entrance of the ravine. The plan was risky, but it was their best chance at turning the tide of the battle. They had intentionally led the Russians here, knowing that the natural landscape would create the perfect ambush point.

"Everything's in place, Colonel," said Captain Mark Jennings, one of Dill's most trusted officers. He had been instrumental in coordinating the movements of the more significant force now closing in on the Russians from all sides.

"Good," Dill replied, his voice steady despite the tension in the air. **"Make sure the men are ready. Once the Russians are fully inside the ravine, we hit them with everything we've got."**

Jennings nodded; his face grim. **"Understood, sir. But what if they realize it's a trap before we're ready?"**

"They won't," Dill said with certainty. **"They're too arrogant, too sure of their victory. They won't see it coming until it's too late."**

The American forces had spent days preparing for this moment, carefully positioning themselves around the ravine, hidden from view. They had brought in a massive reinforcement of 90,000 men, including infantry, artillery, and air support. The Russians had no idea what was waiting for them.

The Trap is Sprung

As the last Russian soldiers entered the ravine, Petrov allowed himself a moment of satisfaction. The Americans were trapped, and soon, they would be nothing more than a memory. He raised his hand to give the order to close in on the remaining American forces when the ground beneath them seemed to erupt in fire and fury.

The first explosion took out an entire platoon of Russian soldiers, sending bodies flying into the air like ragdolls. Chaos erupted as more explosions followed, ripping through the Russian ranks. The air was filled with the deafening roar of artillery shells and the screams of the wounded.

"What the hell is happening?!" Petrov shouted, his voice barely audible over the din.

"They've set traps!" Ivanov yelled, his face pale with shock. **"It's an ambush!"**

Petrov's mind raced. How could this have happened? How had the Americans outsmarted them? But there was no time to think, only to react. He barked orders to his men, trying to regroup and mount a defenses, but it was already too late.

From the ridges above, the American forces opened fire with a relentless barrage of machine guns, mortars, and sniper rifles. The Russians, trapped in the narrow confines of the ravine, had nowhere to run. They were being slaughtered.

"Pull back! Pull back!" Petrov screamed, but his voice was lost in the chaos. His men were panicking, trying to retreat, but they were being cut down before they could make it to safety.

The Destruction of the Russian Forces

Colonel Dill watched the carnage unfold from his command post; his expression unreadable. This was war, brutal and unforgiving. He knew this battle would be remembered for its savagery, but it was necessary. The Russians had to be stopped, and this was the only way.

"Push forward," Dill ordered, his voice calm and controlled. **"Don't let any of them escape."**

The sound was deafening, the air thick with the stench of gunpowder and blood. The once-proud Russian soldiers were now nothing more than targets; their disciplined ranks shattered; their morale crushed.

In the center of the ravine, General Petrov fought desperately to regain control of his forces. He fired his pistol at the advancing Americans, rallying his men to make a final stand, but it was futile. The Americans were relentless, their superior numbers and firepower overwhelming the Russians.

"General, we have to retreat!" Ivanov shouted, grabbing Petrov's arm. "We're being slaughtered!"

"There's nowhere to retreat to!" Petrov snarled, yanking his arm free. **"We fight or we die!"**

But even as he spoke, Petrov knew the battle was lost. The Russians were being cut down in droves, their bodies piling up in the narrow confines of the ravine. The once-clear stream that ran through the center of the ravine was now stained red with blood.

The Final Confrontation

As the battle raged, Colonel Dill led a small contingent of men into the heart of the ravine, determined to capture or kill General Petrov. He knew that taking out the Russian commander would break what little remained of the enemy's resistance.

"Stay sharp," Dill said as they moved through the smoke-filled battlefield. **"Petrov's not going to go down without a fight."**

They moved cautiously, picking their way through the carnage. The sounds of battle were still intense, but the Russian resistance was weakening. Dill could see the fear and desperation in the eyes of the remaining Russian soldiers as they fought on, knowing they were doomed.

"**There!**" one of Dill's men shouted, pointing to a group of Russian officers huddled behind a cluster of rocks. Among them, Dill spotted Petrov, his face twisted in rage and defiance.

"**Take them out!**" Dill ordered, raising his rifle.

The Americans opened fire, cutting down the Russian officers one by one. Petrov, realizing that the end was near, stood his ground, firing his pistol at the advancing Americans. He knew he wouldn't survive, but he was determined to take as many of the enemy with him as he could.

Dill aimed carefully and squeezed the trigger. The bullet struck Petrov in the chest, and the Russian general staggered back, blood pouring from the wound. He fell to his knees, still clutching his pistol, his eyes locked on Dill.

"**You may have won this battle**," Petrov gasped, his voice weak. "**But the war is far from over.**"

Dill approached, his rifle still trained on Petrov. He could see the life fading from the Russian general's eyes, but he knew that Petrov was right. This battle was just one of many in a war that would continue to rage on.

"**Maybe**," Dill said quietly. "**But this is where you die.**"

With that, Dill fired one last shot, ending Petrov's life. The Russian general collapsed to the ground, his blood pooling around him, his pistol falling from his hand.

The Aftermath

The battle of the ravine was over. The Russian forces had been decimated, their once-formidable army reduced to a broken and defeated remnant. The Americans, though victorious, had paid a heavy price. The ground was littered with the bodies of the fallen, both Russian and American, and the ravine itself had become a mass grave.

Colonel Dill stood among the dead, his face grim as he surveyed the aftermath of the battle. This victory had been hard-won, but it was a necessary step in the long and brutal war against the occupying forces. The Russians had underestimated the resolve of the American military, and they had paid the ultimate price.

"Gather the men," Dill ordered Jennings, who had joined him in the ravine. **"We need to regroup and prepare for the next campaign phase."**

Jennings nodded, his face pale but determined. **"Yes, sir. But what about the survivors?"**

Dill looked at the few remaining Russian soldiers who had surrendered, their weapons discarded, their faces hollow with defeat.

"Round them up," Dill said, his voice cold. **"We'll see if they have any helpful information."**

The Naval Clash: A Tale of Grit and Strategy

The Calm Before the Storm

The ocean stretched out in all directions, an endless expanse of dark blue, its surface deceptively calm under the grey skies. The fleet of American warships moved in tight formation, their sleek hulls slicing through the water with purpose. This was the calm before the storm—a quiet moment before the full fury of battle would be unleashed.

On the bridge of the USS **Constellation**, the flagship of the American naval force, Admiral Jim Beasley stood with his hands clasped behind his back, his eyes fixed on the horizon. The tension in the air was palpable, and every crew member was aware of the impending clash with the enemy fleet approaching from the east.

"**Admiral, radar contact confirmed**," said Commander Linda Graham, the ship's executive officer. "**Multiple enemy vessels, approximately 20 nautical miles out, closing fast.**"

Admiral Beasley nodded, his expression unreadable. "**Prepare for battle stations. All ships must maintain formation and hold fire until we have a clear shot.**"

"**Aye, sir**," Graham responded, her voice steady despite the moment's weight. She relayed the orders over the ship's intercom, her voice echoing through the steel corridors.

Below deck, the crew moved efficiently, donning their battle gear and preparing the ship for combat. The hum of machinery, the clatter of boots on metal, and the low murmur of voices filled the air as they made their final preparations.

In the combat information center (CIC), the heart of the ship's operations, screens flickered with data, and the air was thick with tension. The radar display showed a cluster of red dots—enemy ships—moving steadily toward the American fleet. The battle was imminent, and everyone knew it.

First Contact

The first shots of the battle were fired from the USS **Montgomery**, a guided-missile destroyer positioned at the edge of the American formation. The ship's captain, Captain John Reynolds, had been monitoring the enemy's movements closely, waiting for the right moment to strike.

"**Enemy ships are within range**," reported the tactical officer, his eyes locked on the targeting screen. "**Permission to engage?**"

"**Permission granted**," Captain Reynolds said, his voice calm. "**Fire at will.**"

The **Montgomery's** vertical launch systems roared to life, sending a volley of Tomahawk missiles streaking into the sky. The missiles arced high over the water, their engines leaving a trail of smoke as they sped toward the enemy fleet.

"**Missiles away**," the tactical officer confirmed. "**Impact in thirty seconds.**"

On the bridge of the USS **Constellation**, Admiral Beasley watched the missile contrails disappear into the distance. "**The enemy knows we're here now**," he said, almost to himself. "**Let's see how they respond.**"

The response came quickly. The enemy fleet, a formidable force of Russian and Chinese warships, began to return fire, launching their missiles in a counterattack. The sky above the ocean was soon filled with streaks of light as the two forces exchanged volleys, the air thick with the sounds of engines and the distant booms of explosions.

"**Enemy missiles incoming!**" Commander Graham shouted, her eyes on the radar display. "**Brace for impact!**"

The **Constellation's** defensive systems kicked into high gear. Phalanx close-in weapon systems (CIWS) whirred to life, their rapid-fire guns spewing streams of tracer rounds into the air, trying to intercept the incoming missiles. Anti-missile countermeasures were deployed, sending flares and chaff into the sky in a desperate attempt to confuse the enemy's targeting systems.

"**Hold steady!**" Admiral Beasley commanded, his voice cutting through the chaos. "**Focus on the task at hand!**"

The first enemy missile struck the water just off the port side of the **Constellation**, sending up a massive plume of water. The ship rocked violently, but the crew held their ground, their training kicking in as they continued to man their stations.

"**Damage report!**" Beasley called out, his eyes never leaving the battle unfolding before him.

"**Minor damage to port side, no casualties,**" the damage control officer reported. "**All systems are operational.**"

Beasley nodded, his face set in a grim expression. "**Good. Keep up the pressure. We're not out of this yet.**"

The Battle Intensifies

As the battle raged, the ocean became a cauldron of fire and steel. The two fleets were now fully engaged, with ships on both sides exchanging deadly fire. The air was thick with the smell of burning fuel and the acrid stench of cordite, the sounds of explosions and the screech of metal on metal creating a deafening din.

On the bridge of the **Montgomery**, Captain Reynolds was in the thick of the action, precisely directing his ship's movements. The destroyer weaved through the water, evading enemy fire while unleashing devastating attacks.

"**Target the lead ship in the enemy formation,**" Reynolds ordered. "**Let's take out their command and control.**"

The **Montgomery's** guns roared to life, sending a barrage of shells toward the enemy flagship, a massive Russian cruiser. The shells struck home, punching through the ship's thick armour and sending flames and smoke billowing into the sky.

"**Direct hit!**" the tactical officer reported, a note of triumph in his voice.

"**Good work**," Reynolds said, his eyes narrowing as he surveyed the battlefield. "**But we're not done yet. Keep the pressure on them.**"

Meanwhile, aboard the USS **Roosevelt**, an aircraft carrier serving as the centerpiece of the American fleet, Captain Sarah Mitchell was coordinating air operations with the precision of a conductor leading an orchestra. The carrier's deck was a hive of activity, with fighter jets and attack helicopters taking off and landing continuously.

"**Launch the next wave of sorties**," Mitchell ordered, her voice calm despite the intensity of the battle. "**Focus on their missile platforms. We need to neutralize their long-range capabilities.**"

The deck crews moved with practiced efficiency, loading weapons and refuelling the jets as they prepared for their next mission. Within minutes, a squadron of F-35 Lightning IIs roared into the sky, their afterburners glowing as they streaked toward the enemy fleet.

In **Roosevelt's CIC**, the air operations officer monitored the strike group's progress, flicking his eyes between the radar screens and the communication channels.

"**Strike group is approaching the target**," he reported. "**Enemy anti-aircraft fire is heavy, but they're pressing on.**"

"**Keep them focused**," Captain Mitchell said. "**They know what's at stake.**"

Communication Breakdown

As the battle dragged on, the intensity of the fighting began to take its toll on both sides. Ships were heavily damaged, some sinking into the cold depths of the ocean, their crews desperately abandoning ship as the water closed in around them.

The American fleet was holding its own, but the enemy was relentless, their sheer numbers threatening to overwhelm the defenders. Admiral Beasley knew that the battle's outcome could hinge on a single moment, mistake, or luck that could tip the scales in either direction.

"**Admiral, we're getting interference on the comms,**" Commander Graham reported, her brow furrowed as she adjusted the radio dials. "**It's getting harder to coordinate with the other ships.**"

"Jamming?" Beasley asked, his eyes narrowing.

"**Possibly,**" Graham replied. "**But it could also be the sheer volume of signals. The enemy is using every frequency they can to disrupt our communications.**"

Beasley frowned. Communication was the lifeblood of naval warfare, and without it, their ability to coordinate and execute complex maneuvers would be severely compromised.

"**Get the EW (Electronic Warfare) team on it**," Beasley ordered. "**I want those channels cleared.**"

Down in the bowels of the **Constellation**, the EW team sprang into action. They worked feverishly to counteract the enemy's jamming efforts, trying to clear the communication channels and restore the flow of information between the ships.

"**Sir, we're getting some signals through**," reported Lieutenant Daniels, the head of the EW team. "**But it's spotty at best. We might need to switch to backup frequencies.**"

"**Do it,**" Beasley said. "**And get word to the other ships. We need to stay in contact.**"

The battle continued, with the American ships holding their ground despite the growing pressure from the enemy fleet. However, the communication problems persisted, causing delays and confusion as the commanders struggled to relay orders to their crews.

Turning the Tide

As the battle reached its climax, the American fleet was on the verge of being overwhelmed. The enemy was closing in, their ships pressing the attack with unrelenting ferocity. But Admiral Beasley had one last card to play.

"Prepare for a coordinated strike," Beasley ordered, his voice steely with determination. **"All ships are to target the enemy's command vessels. We're going to decapitate their leadership."**

The orders were relayed through the now-cleared communication channels, and the American ships prepared for one final, all-out assault. The crews knew this was their last chance to turn the tide of the battle, and they steeled themselves for the task ahead.

"On my mark," Beasley said, echoing through the bridge. **"Three... two... one... fire!"**

The American ships unleashed a devastating barrage of missiles, torpedoes, and gunfire, all aimed at the heart of the enemy fleet. The sky was filled with the glow of explosions as multiple hits struck the enemy command ships, their hulls ripped open by the relentless.

Battle at Sea: The Clash of Titans

The actual battle raged in the cold depths of the Pacific, where sunlight barely penetrates. New America's Navy, equipped with advanced stealth technology, strategically positioned its submarines, creating an invisible net around the enemy fleet. These submarines, ghosts of the deep, were armed with the latest torpedoes and equipped with sonar systems so advanced that they could detect even the faintest movements miles away.

The Submarine Involvement:

Leading the New American submarine fleet was the USS Silent Shadow, a state-of-the-art nuclear-powered submarine captained by Commander Ethan Hayes. Hayes, a veteran of countless underwater skirmishes, knew that the success of this battle hinged on stealth, precision, and timing.

"We've got them where we want them," Hayes muttered to his crew, eyes fixed on the sonar display. The blips on the screen marked the positions of the Russian and Chinese submarines lurking just beyond the enemy fleet, waiting to strike.

Commander Hayes ordered the Silent Shadow to move into position, gliding silently through the water like a shark ready to pounce. Meanwhile, the USS Viper and USS Black Tide, two other New American submarines, began a flanking maneuver to encircle the enemy from the sides.

Above the surface, the New American surface fleet, led by Admiral Jim Beasley, began engaging the enemy ships. Missiles streaked through the sky, and the thunderous roar of naval guns echoed across the ocean. But this was merely a feint to distract the enemy from the threat lurking below.

As the surface battle intensified, the Silent Shadow moved into striking distance. The crew held their breath as the target, a massive Chinese aircraft carrier, appeared on the screen. It was heavily guarded, surrounded by destroyers and frigates, but Commander Hayes knew that the element of surprise was on their side.

"Fire torpedoes," Hayes ordered, his voice calm but filled with determination.

The Silent Shadow launched its first volley of torpedoes, streaking through the water with deadly precision. Moments later, the Viper and Black Tide followed suit, their torpedoes aimed at the enemy destroyers and submarines. The ocean erupted in chaos as explosions ripped through the enemy fleet. The Chinese aircraft carrier shuddered as multiple torpedoes slammed into its hull, tearing through the metal and sending it listing to one side.

The Russians and Chinese, caught off guard by the ferocity of the underwater assault, scrambled to respond. Their submarines, now aware of the New American presence, launched counterattacks, but it was too late. The Silent Shadow and its counterparts had already repositioned, vanishing back into the depths like specters.

A Russian submarine, the K-525, managed to get a lock on the Viper, launching a torpedo in retaliation. The Viper's crew reacted instantly, deploying countermeasures and executing evasive maneuvers. The enemy torpedo passed harmlessly by, detonating in the open water.

Commander Hayes, watching the battle unfold, knew that this was their moment to turn the tide. The Silent Shadow targeted another enemy submarine, the Chinese Ming-class vessel, and fired. The torpedo struck true, and the explosion tore the enemy submarine apart and sank to the ocean floor.

The Turning Point:

With the enemy submarines crippled and their surface fleet in disarray, New America's forces seized the upper hand. The surface ships, now free from the threat of underwater attack, pressed their advantage. The remnants of the Russian and Chinese fleets attempted a retreat, but the New American submarines were relentless.

In a final act of defiance, the Silent Shadow surfaced, revealing itself to the enemy fleet. Commander Hayes ordered one last salvo of torpedoes as the Russian and Chinese ships turned their guns on it. The Silent Shadow fired, its torpedoes finding their mark on a Russian cruiser, which erupted in a fiery explosion.

As the battle drew close, the once mighty enemy fleet lay in ruins, the survivors fleeing to their distant shores. Having fulfilled their mission, the New American submarines slipped back into the depths, their work done.

The Battle of the Pacific had been won, not through brute force, but through the cunning and skill of the submariners who had turned the ocean into their battlefield. The seas now belonged to New America, and with this victory, the tide of war began to shift in their favour.

The Deception Unfolds

The aftermath of the naval battle was a tense time for New America and its enemies. The ocean waves still bore the scars of the recent clash, with debris from sunken ships and the bodies of the fallen floating like grim reminders of the cost of war. The victory at sea had shifted the balance of power, but an uneasy tension lurked in the shadow of triumph. The prisoners—the leaders of Russia, China, and North Korea—remained in the custody of New America. These men, responsible for untold suffering and destruction, were not ordinary prisoners of war; they were symbols of a conflict that had torn the world apart.

New America's leadership faced a difficult decision. The pressure to do something with these high-profile captives was mounting. The world watched closely, with allies and enemies eager to see what would come next. For many, the idea of holding such dangerous figures indefinitely was fraught with risk. The longer they remained in New American custody, the more their supporters would rally for their release and the greater the chance of a retaliatory strike.

Amid this uncertainty, an agreement was reached. The captured leaders would be exchanged and released under the condition that they leave American soil and never return. It was a calculated decision, a diplomatic move meant to avoid further escalation. The terms were clear: the leaders would be returned to their respective countries, and the hostilities would cease in exchange. It was a fragile truce that offered a glimmer of hope in an otherwise bleak landscape.

In the days leading up to the exchange, a tense calm settled over New America. The captured leaders—Vladimir Petrov, General Xiang, and Supreme Leader Kim—were kept under heavy guard in a secure facility. The deal had been brokered with the understanding that the leaders would adhere to their word, leave America behind, and end their aggression. But there was something in their eyes, a cold calculation that belied their outward compliance.

The exchange was set to occur on a remote airstrip, far from prying eyes. The location had been chosen for its isolation, where the transfer could be conducted without interference. As the day approached, a sense of unease permeated the air. Intelligence reports had been mixed—some suggested that the enemy was regrouping, while others indicated a genuine willingness to retreat. The truth, however, was far more sinister.

On the morning of the exchange, the skies were overcast, with grey clouds hanging low over the horizon. A convoy of armoured vehicles arrived at the airstrip, carrying the three leaders. Elite New American forces flanked them, their faces obscured by helmets and visors. The soldiers were on high alert, scanning the surroundings for any sign of betrayal.

The enemy planes arrived shortly after, landing with a roar on the cracked tarmac. As agreed, a small contingent of unarmed soldiers emerged from each aircraft. They approached slowly, their movements deliberate and controlled. There was a brief exchange of words between the commanders on both sides, followed by a tense silence as the leaders were escorted across the airstrip.

As the leaders reached their respective planes, they turned back to face their captors, a faint smirk playing on their lips. Something about how they carried themselves—their confidence, their assuredness—sent a chill down the spine of everyone present. It was as if they knew something that the New Americans did not.

The planes departed, engines roaring as they lifted off the ground and disappeared into the clouds. The exchange was over. The leaders were gone. For a moment, it seemed peace might be within reach.

But the sense of relief was short-lived. Hours after the exchange, reports began to filter in—disturbing reports that hinted at a betrayal. The enemy had not retreated. Instead, their forces were regrouping, their warships and aircraft repositioning for a new assault. It was clear: the leaders had lied. They had never intended to leave America in peace.

Back in New America, the realization hit like a hammer blow. The exchange had been a ruse, a clever deception designed to buy the enemy time to reorganize and prepare for their next move. The leaders had played their part flawlessly, and now they were back in command, directing their forces with renewed vigor.

The betrayal sparked a flurry of activity within New America's military and intelligence communities. The enemy's forces were moving, and it was only a matter of time before they struck again. The high command convened an emergency meeting to discuss their next steps. The stakes had never been higher, and the margin for error was razor thin.

Tensions ran high in the war room as the leaders of New America grappled with the implications of the enemy's betrayal. Maps and charts covered the walls, showing the latest intelligence on enemy movements. The grim reality was that the war was far from over. The enemy had gained a crucial advantage, and it would take every ounce of New America's strength and resolve to turn the tide once more.

In the days that followed, the situation deteriorated rapidly. The enemy's forces launched a series of coordinated attacks, striking at crucial military installations and infrastructure across New America. The assaults were brutal and relentless, catching the defenders off guard. The enemy had been preparing for this moment and determined to make the most of it.

For New America, the situation was dire. The betrayal had shaken the nation's confidence, and the threat of invasion loomed large. But even in the face of overwhelming odds, the spirit of resistance burned brightly. The leaders of New America knew they could not afford to falter now. They would have to regroup, adapt, and fight back with everything they had.

As the nation braced for the coming storm, a sense of resolve took hold. The betrayal had been a harsh lesson, a reminder that the enemy could not be trusted. But it had also ignited a fire within New America, a determination to defend their homeland at all costs. The battle for America's future was far from over, and the fight was only beginning.

The Air and Land Battle

89

The First Cavalry and Second Armoured Division Join the Fight

The news of the enemy's betrayal spread like wildfire through New America's military ranks. The hard-fought victories at sea now seemed almost hollow as the realization sank in—the war was far from over.

But the nation's resolve grew more robust in the face of this renewed threat. Reinforcements were mobilized, and at the forefront of this new wave of strength were the legendary First Cavalry Division and the Second Armoured Division, both ready to join the fray and turn the tide once more.

In the heart of Texas, the First Cavalry Division, known for its storied history and unmatched versatility, was preparing to deploy. Soldiers moved with purpose; their faces grim but determined. The roar of engines filled the air as helicopters were prepped for take-off, and tanks rumbled across the tarmac, their heavy treads crushing the earth beneath them.

Colonel Robert Anderson, a seasoned veteran who had seen combat in some of the most hostile environments, stood before his men. His tall, imposing figure commanded respect, and his voice carried the weight of experience.

"Men, we've done it," Anderson said, his voice filled with emotion. "The enemy is on the run. We've shown them what the First Cavalry is made of. But this fight isn't over yet. We need to secure the area and make sure they don't regroup. Stay sharp, and let's finish this." He paused, letting his words sink in as he scanned the faces of his soldiers, each one hardened by years of training and battle.

"We are the First Cavalry Division," Anderson continued, his tone steely. "We have a legacy of fighting against the odds, of standing our ground when no one else can. This is our time to

remind the world who we are. We're going to show those bastards that they messed with the wrong country."

The soldiers responded with a unified roar, their voices echoing the camp. Anderson nodded, satisfied with their resolve.

"We'll be moving out within the hour," he said. "Get your gear squared away, check your equipment, and be ready to move immediately. This fight isn't easy, but I do not doubt that every one of you is ready. Let's make them regret the day they crossed paths with the First Cav."

As the men dispersed to prepare, Anderson turned to his XO, Major Sarah Reed, a sharp-minded officer who had proven herself in countless operations.

"Reed, I want our air support to be on point," Anderson said, his voice low but urgent. "Those birds are going to be our lifeline out there. We can't afford any mistakes."

"Understood, sir," Reed replied, already moving to relay the orders. "I'll make sure they're ready to go."

Meanwhile, in the rolling plains of Kansas, the Second Armoured Division was making final preparations for deployment. The division, known as "Hell on Wheels," was a force to be reckoned with, its tanks and armoured vehicles ready to bring the fight to the enemy in a way that only they could.

Communication from the Commanders:

Brigadier General Marcus Hayes, commander of the Second Armoured Division, stood atop a command vehicle, his eyes scanning the sea of men and machines before him. Hayes spoke few words, but when he said, his men listened.

"Men, we've been called into action," Hayes began, his voice carrying over the rumble of engines. "Our country is under attack, and it's our job to ensure that those responsible pay the price. We've faced tough enemies before, but this time, we're up against a foe who thinks they can outmaneuver and outgun us. I say let them try."

He paused, his gaze hardening as he looked out at the faces of his men—soldiers who had served with him through thick and thin.

"We are the Second Armoured," Hayes continued, his voice growing stronger. **"We don't back down. We don't run. When the enemy sees us coming, they know they're in for a world of hurt. That's exactly what we're going to deliver."**

There was a murmur of agreement among the troops, their confidence in their commander unshakable.

"We're rolling out as soon as the order comes down," Hayes said. **"I want every tank, every APC, every piece of equipment ready to go. This will be a fight to the finish, and I expect nothing less than your absolute best."**

He stepped down from the vehicle, giving a final nod to his men before heading toward the command center. As he walked, his second-in-command, Colonel David Ramirez, fell into step beside him.

"Ramirez," Hayes said, his voice low, **"I want you to coordinate with the First Cav. We're going to be working closely with them on this. Ensure we're in sync; there's no room for error."**

"Got it, General," Ramirez replied. **"I'll make sure we're locked in with their movements."** Hayes nodded, his mind already racing ahead to the battle to come. He knew the stakes were high, but he also knew his men were ready. The Second Armoured Division was about to show the enemy what Hell on Wheels meant.

As the final preparations were made, the two divisions began to converge on the front lines. The First Cavalry, with its helicopters and light armour, would provide rapid response and mobility. At the same time, the Second Armoured, with its heavy tanks and artillery, would bring the hammer down on any enemy forces that dared to stand in their way. Together, they were a formidable force, a combination of speed, firepower, and tactical brilliance that would strike fear into the hearts of their enemies.

The Battle Begins

As the sun dipped below the horizon, casting long shadows over the battlefield, the First Cavalry Division and the Second Armoured Division moved into position. The terrain was rough, a mixture of rolling hills and dense forest that would test even the most seasoned soldiers. But these men and women were ready; they had trained for this, prepared for every eventuality. Now, it was time to put that training to the test.

The First Cavalry Division was the first to engage. Using their helicopters to traverse the uneven terrain quickly, they established forward operating bases, creating a network of outposts to serve as staging grounds for the coming assault. The light armour and infantry moved precisely, setting up defensive positions and securing key routes for the heavier forces that would follow.

Colonel Anderson stood in the command tent, a battlefield map appearing before him. His senior officers gathered around him; their faces set with determination.

"We're going to hit them hard and fast," Anderson said, tracing a line across the map. **"The enemy expects us to come at them head-on, but we'll outflank them. Our air support will soften their positions, and then we'll move in to finish the job."**

Major Reed nodded, her eyes scanning the map. **"Our scouts have identified several weak points in their lines. If we can exploit those, we can cut them off from their supply lines and force them into a retreat."**

"Exactly," Anderson replied. **"Timing is crucial here. We'll coordinate with the Second Armoured, ensuring they can deliver the knockout punch once we've broken through."**

He looked around at his officers, his expression serious. **"This will be a tough fight, but I do not doubt we'll come out on top. Get your men ready—we move at first light."**

As the First Cavalry prepared for their assault, the Second Armoured Division was also making its final preparations. The heavy tanks and artillery of "Hell on Wheels" were a fearsome sight, their engines rumbling like distant thunder as they moved into position. Brigadier General Hayes knew that his division would be the hammer in this operation, delivering crushing blows to the enemy forces once the First Cavalry had broken through.

General Hayes stood on a rise overlooking the battlefield, his binoculars trained on the enemy positions in the distance. Beside him stood Colonel Ramirez, his second-in-command.

"Ramirez, what's the status of our armour?" Hayes asked, his voice calm but commanding.

"All units are in position, sir," Ramirez replied. **"Tanks are ready to move, and the artillery is set to begin bombardment as soon as we get the go-ahead."**

"Good," Hayes said, lowering his binoculars. **"The First Cavalry is going to soften them up for us, but we're the ones who will finish this. Once they've created an opening, we'll drive straight through their lines and crush them before they can regroup."**

He turned to Ramirez; his eyes steely. **"I want our men to be ready for anything. The enemy is desperate—they know that if they lose here, it's over for them. We must be prepared for counterattacks, ambushes, anything they can throw at us."**

"We'll be ready, sir," Ramirez said confidently.

Hayes nodded, satisfied. **"Then let's get to it. We move out as soon as the signal comes through."**

As the night wore on, the soldiers of both divisions settled into their positions, checking and rechecking their equipment, mentally preparing themselves for the battle ahead. There was a tense silence over the battlefield, broken only by the distant sound of engines and the occasional murmur of voices.

At dawn, the order came through. The First Cavalry Division launched its assault, helicopters swooping low over the trees, their rotors slicing through the air. The ground forces moved in tandem, advancing quickly on the enemy positions. The initial attack caught the enemy off guard, their forward defensess crumbling under the relentless assault.

Colonel Anderson was in the thick of it, coordinating the assault from a forward command post. His radio crackled with reports from the field, the voices of his officers coming through with urgent updates.

"Alpha Company, we've breached the first line of defenses," one of the officers reported. "Resistance is heavier than expected, but we're holding our ground."

"Roger that, Alpha," Anderson replied. "Keep pushing forward. We need to break through their second line before they can regroup. Air support is on the way to clear a path."

He switched channels and connected to Major Reed. "Reed, what's the status of the airstrike?"

"They're en route, sir," Reed replied. "ETA is five minutes. We're coordinating with artillery to ensure maximum impact."

"Good," Anderson said. "Once that strike hits, I want all units to move in immediately. We must keep the pressure on and not give them a chance to recover."

As the First Cavalry continued their assault, the Second Armoured Division began to move. The ground shook as the tanks rolled forward, their massive turrets swiveling to track enemy targets. Artillery rained down on the enemy positions, sending plumes of dirt and smoke into the air. The enemy forces, already reeling from the initial attack, struggled to mount a coherent defenses.

General Hayes was in his command vehicle, monitoring the battle through screens and radio transmissions. His face was a mask of concentration as he directed his forces with the precision of a seasoned strategist.

"**All units advance to phase two positions,**" Hayes ordered. "**Tanks, keep your formation tight—we don't want to give them any openings. Artillery, maintain suppression fire on their flanks. We're going to punch through their center and drive them back.**"

His radio crackled as reports came in from the front lines. One of his officers reported. "**They're trying to regroup.**"

"**Engage them, General. Enemy armoured vehicles spotted ahead,**" Hayes replied without hesitation. Take out their armour before they can form a defensive line. We can't afford to let them stall our advance."

The tanks of the Second Armoured Division surged forward, their guns blazing as they engaged the enemy armor. The battle was fierce, with both sides exchanging heavy fire. But the Second Armoured's superior training and coordination began to tip the scales in New America's favor. One by one, the enemy tanks were destroyed, their hulks left smouldering on the battlefield.

As the battle raged on, the First Cavalry and Second Armoured continued to work in tandem, their combined might overwhelming the enemy forces. The enemy began to falter, now cut off from their supply lines and surrounded. Their morale, already shaken by the relentless assault, was shattered as the full might of New America's military bore down on them.

In the final stages of the battle, the enemy attempted a desperate counterattack, throwing everything they had left at the advancing forces. But it was too little, too late. The First Cavalry, with their mobility and air support, quickly confused the enemy, while the Second Armoured Division crushed their remaining forces with brutal efficiency.

Colonel Anderson watched as the enemy lines crumbled, his heart swelling with pride. He keyed his radio and addressed his entire division.

"Men, we've done it," Anderson said, his voice filled with emotion. "The enemy is on the run. We've shown them what the First Cavalry is made of. But this fight isn't over yet. We need to secure the area and make sure they don't regroup. Stay sharp, and let's finish this." At the same time, General Hayes was giving orders like his men's. "This is it, boys," he said, his voice carrying over the roar of battle. "We've broken them. Now, we're going to chase them down and make sure they never threaten our country again. Keep your eyes open, and let's bring this home."

The battle ended in a decisive victory for New America. The combined forces of the First Cavalry Division and the Second Armoured Division repelled the enemy and destroyed their ability to continue the fight. The enemy's betrayal was costly, but New America's resolve and determination prevailed in the end.

The battlefield was quiet now, the smoke slowly clearing to reveal the devastation that had been wrought. Tanks stood victorious on the blood-soaked ground, their guns still smoking. Soldiers moved among the wreckage, securing the area and tending to the wounded. The enemy, those who had survived, had been captured or had fled into the wilderness, their forces shattered beyond repair.

America Last Stand

The Battle of the Ridge

The smoke still lingered in the air, a choking reminder of the devastation unfolding. The 2nd Armoured Division had fought with the ferocity of lions, smashing through the enemy lines with the precision and power of a well-oiled war machine. The echoes of cannon fire, the roar of engines, and the cries of wounded men still resonated in the minds of the soldiers who had survived the brutal encounter. But the battle was far from over.

Colonel James "Iron Hide" Williams, the commanding officer of the 2nd Armoured, peered through his binoculars at the ridge ahead. His weathered face, marked by years of combat, showed little emotion as he scanned the horizon. His steely blue eyes, however, betrayed a deep concern that only a seasoned warrior could recognize. He knew what was coming.

"Colonel, we've got movement on the ridge!" shouted Lieutenant Jacobs, his voice strained with urgency. The young officer was barely out of his twenties but had already seen enough battle to last a lifetime.

Williams lowered his binoculars and turned to his XO, Major Samuel Carter. **"Get the men ready, Sam. We're about to have company."**

Carter nodded, understanding the gravity of the situation without a word. He immediately began barking orders to the platoon leaders, rallying the troops for the impending assault.

Through the haze of smoke and dust, the enemy emerged, a sight that sent a chill down the spine of every soldier present. The Russian tanks, sleek and menacing, rolled over the ridge like a tide of steel. These weren't the remnants of a broken force—they were fresh, reinforced, and driven by a singular purpose: vengeance.

Behind the armoured vehicles, the elite Spetsnaz troops moved with lethal precision, their black uniforms stark against the barren landscape. They were ghosts, trained to strike with speed and brutality, and their presence alone was enough to unsettle even the most hardened veterans.

"**Incoming!**" The warning rang out across the comms as the first barrage of artillery shells exploded in the distance, sending plumes of dirt and fire skyward. The ground trembled under the force of the impact, and the soldiers of the 2nd Armoured braced themselves for the onslaught.

Williams climbed into the turret of his Abrams tank, gripping the controls with white-knuckled intensity. "**All units, hold the line! Do not let them break through!**"

The radio crackled with acknowledgments as the division's tanks formed a defensive perimeter, their cannons trained on the approaching enemy. The air was thick with tension, every man and woman knowing that this would be a fight to the death.

The Russian tanks charged forward, their engines roaring like angry beasts. The first volley of tank shells was fired, a deafening symphony of destruction as the 2nd Armoured unleashed its fury. Shells ripped through the air, finding their targets with deadly accuracy. Explosions rocked the battlefield as enemy tanks were obliterated in fiery blasts; their hulks were left soldering in the aftermath.

But the Russians kept coming, undeterred by the losses. Their determination was terrifying, driven by a desire to avenge their fallen comrades. As they advanced, the Spetsnaz troops darted between the vehicles, using the armoured beasts as cover. They were fast, ruthless, and utterly fearless.

Williams felt the tank shudder as it took a hit, the armor holding but the impact rattling his bones. "Return fire! Keep them off us!"

The gunner responded instantly, the Abrams cannon spitting fire as it engaged the closest Russian tank. The round struck true, and the enemy vehicle erupted in a flame. But there was no time to celebrate—the battle was chaos, a maelstrom of destruction where victory and defeat hung by the thinnest threads.

Suddenly, the Spetsnaz were among them. The elite Russian soldiers had closed the distance with terrifying speed, and now they were inside the 2nd Armorer's lines. They moved with precision, throwing grenades and firing automatic weapons with deadly accuracy. Tanks were disabled as grenades were tossed into their hatches, the explosions turning the armoured beasts into burning coffins.

Williams knew they were in trouble. **"All units, fall back to the secondary position! Regroup and hold your ground!"**

The order was given, and the tanks began to reverse, firing as they went. But the Spetsnaz were relentless, their assault coordinated and brutal. They were like wolves among sheep, brutally cutting down any resistance.

Major Carter's voice came over the radio, calm but urgent. **"Colonel, we're getting overrun! We need air support, now!"**

Williams cursed under his breath. The skies had been contested all day, with enemy aircraft making it nearly impossible to get close air support. But they needed more options.

"Command, this is Iron hide. We need air support at grid 4-7-8. We're under heavy assault and falling back. Repeat, we need air support!"

The radio crackled, and there was nothing but static for a moment. Then, finally, the response came. **"Iron hide, this is Eagle One. We're inbound; ETA is five minutes. Hold tight."**

Five minutes. It might as well have been an eternity.

The Day of Reckoning

The dawn of a new day broke over the battlefield, the first rays of sunlight piercing through the lingering smoke and fog that had settled overnight. The once tumultuous landscape, marred by the scars of war, now lay in an eerie silence. The roar of tanks, the thunder of artillery, and the cries of soldiers had all but ceased, replaced by the quiet stillness that follows a hard-fought victory.

General William Shepard stood on the ridge overlooking the valley where the final confrontation occurred. His tattered and stained uniform bore the marks of the grueling campaign, but his posture was as firm as ever. He had led the forces of New America through the darkest hours, and now, at long last, the end was in sight.

Behind him, the remnants of the New American Army gathered, a mixture of hardened veterans and fresh-faced recruits forged in the crucible of battle. Their faces, streaked with dirt and sweat, showed a mix of exhaustion and cautious hope. They had endured much, but they knew this moment was crucial—everything they had fought for hinged on what was about to happen.

"General Shepard," a voice called out, breaking the silence. It was Major Emily Sanchez, one of Shepard's most trusted officers. **"The enemy delegation is approaching."**

Shepard nodded, his gaze never leaving the horizon. **"Let them come."**

A convoy of enemy vehicles appeared from the valley's far side, their white flags of surrender stark against the backdrop of devastation. The sight was almost surreal; the same forces that had once driven deep into the heart of America, spreading terror and destruction, were now humbled, their weapons lowered in a show of submission.

As the convoy came to a stop, a group of high-ranking enemy officers disembarked, their expressions a mixture of defeat and resignation. Leading them was General Mikhail Petrov, the commander of the Russian forces, flanked by his Chinese and North Korean counterparts. These men had once been the architects of a brutal invasion, but now, they were little more than shadows of their former selves.

Shepard stepped forward, his eyes locked on Petrov's. There was no need for words between them; the weight of history was palpable. The two generals stared at one another for a moment, silently acknowledging the cost of the war between their nations.

Finally, Petrov broke the silence. **"General Shepard, we come to you under the flag of surrender. Our forces are broken, and our supply lines are cut. We have no choice but to accept the terms of your victory."**

Shepard's voice was calm, measured. **"And what terms do you propose, General Petrov?"**

Petrov hesitated the weight of his words pressing down on him. **"We request safe passage out of American territory for all remaining forces. In exchange, we offer the immediate cessation of all hostilities, the release of all prisoners of war, and a full withdrawal of our troops."**

Shepard considered this for a moment, his mind racing through the possibilities. The enemy was defeated, but allowing them to leave without consequence would be a bitter pill for many to swallow. Yet, the prospect of ending the war, of finally bringing peace to a nation that had endured so much, was too powerful to ignore.

"Very well," Shepard said at last. **"We accept your surrender and agree to your terms, with one condition. Your withdrawal must be immediate, and it must be total. Any attempt to stall or leave behind forces will be considered an act of continued aggression and will be met with overwhelming force. Do I make myself clear?"**

Petrov nodded, the relief evident in his eyes. **"Crystal clear, General. You have my word."**

With the formalities complete, Shepard turned to his officers. **"Major Sanchez, see that our troops stand down but remain vigilant. We'll escort the enemy forces to the border and ensure their departure is as swift as promised."**

As Sanchez relayed the orders, Shepard watched the enemy officers closely. His heart had no triumph, no desire to gloat over the vanquished. Instead, he felt a deep weariness that only came after years of relentless struggle. The war had taken its toll on all of them, and though the battle was won, the scars it left behind would take far longer to heal.

The enemy forces began their retreat later that afternoon. It was a slow, methodical process overseen by New American soldiers who lined the roads, their weapons ready. The once-proud invasion force now moved with a sombre discipline, their ranks thinned, and their spirits broken. Tanks that had once rolled across American soil with impunity were now battered and burned, their hulks limping toward the border.

As the last enemy vehicles disappeared, a collective sigh of relief swept through the ranks of the New American Army. The war, it seemed, was finally over. But Shepard knew better than to celebrate prematurely. There was still much work to be done—rebuilding, reuniting, and ensuring such an invasion could never happen again.

He called his officers together; their faces reflecting the same exhaustion and resolve he felt. "This is a victory, but it's not the end. We've won the battle, but now we must win the peace. Our country is in ruins, and it's up to us to rebuild it stronger than before. We must be vigilant, for though the enemy is retreating, the threats we face are far from over."

Major Sanchez stepped forward, her expression one of determination. **"Sir, the men and women under your command are ready. We've faced the worst and come out the other side. Whatever comes next, we'll be ready."**

Shepard nodded, a rare smile tugging at the corners of his mouth. **"I know you will, Major. We all will."**

purpose. The enemy had surrendered, but the road ahead was long and uncertain. Yet, for the first time in years, there was a glimmer of hope—a hope that, despite the darkness, they could reclaim their nation and forge a future worthy of their sacrifices.

CONCLUSION

A Nation Reborn: The Unification of America and the Return to God

The nightmare of foreign occupation and internal strife was over. For the first time in years, the people of the United States could breathe a collective sigh of relief. But this was not just the end of a war—it was the beginning of something far more significant. The United States, once fractured and battered, was now on the cusp of a glorious rebirth. At the heart of this renewal was a return to the principles that had once made the nation great—freedom, unity, and an unyielding faith in God.

The victory had come at a steep price. Countless lives had been lost, cities had been reduced to rubble, and the scars of conflict ran deep across the land. Yet, out of this darkness, a new light began to shine. The leaders of New America, along with the newly liberated states, recognized that the only way forward was together. The time they had come to reunite the fifty states under a single banner, to restore the nation to its former glory, and to rebuild not just with bricks and mortar but with faith and hope.

Reunification Begins:

In the heart of Washington, D.C., the Capitol building stood as a symbol of resilience. Though it had been damaged during the occupation, its dome still reached toward the heavens, a beacon of hope for a weary nation. In the halls of power, it was here that the new leadership of America convened to chart the course for the future. James Alexander, the newly appointed Chair of the National Committee, stood at the podium in the Senate chamber, addressing the gathered representatives of all fifty states.

"**Ladies and gentlemen**," Alexander began, his voice strong and clear, "**we stand today on the threshold of a new era. The trials we have endured, and our sacrifices have brought us to this moment. The United States of America, once divided, is whole again. We are one nation, under God, indivisible, with liberty and justice for all.**"

The chamber erupted in applause, a sound that echoed through the corridors of the Capitol, filling every corner with a renewed purpose. The representatives, many of whom had fought on the front lines or had led their states through the darkest days of the occupation, knew the significance of this moment. They were not just witnessing history—they were making it.

The Return to God:

As the applause subsided, Alexander continued, his tone becoming more solemn. "But as we rebuild our nation, we must not forget the lessons we have learned. Our strength does not come from our military might alone, nor from our wealth or resources. It comes from our faith in each other and God."

He paused, allowing his words to sink in. "**For too long, we have drifted away from the values that once guided us. We allowed ourselves to be consumed by greed, division, and false belief that we could prosper without the guiding hand of the Almighty. But our faith sustained us in our darkest hour, when all seemed lost. It was our prayers that lifted us, and it was God's grace that delivered us from the brink of destruction.**"

Alexander's words resonated deeply with those in the chamber. Many of the representatives had experienced firsthand the power of faith during the war—whether in the quiet moments of prayer before battle, the comfort of a chaplain's words, or the miraculous survival of comrades against all odds. They knew this victory was not theirs alone but a testament to a higher power at work.

A National Day of Prayer:

Alexander proposed a National Day of Prayer and Thanksgiving to commemorate the reunification of the United States and honor the role of faith in their victory. This day would be a time for all Americans to come together, regardless of their background or beliefs, to give thanks for their blessings and rededicate themselves to the principles upon which the nation was founded.

"We will gather in our churches, synagogues, mosques, and homes," Alexander declared. **"We will lift our voices in prayer, asking for God's continued guidance as we embark on this new chapter in our history. And we will remember that it is not by our strength alone that we have triumphed but by the grace of God."**

The proposal was met with overwhelming support, not just in the chamber but across the nation. Churches began preparing for the exceptional services, communities organized gatherings, and families planned to pray together. The unity forged in the crucible of war was now cemented by a shared faith and a collective commitment to putting God first.

The Healing Process:

The reunification of the United States was not just a political or military achievement—it was a ly spiritual journey for the nation. War wounds were still fresh, and the healing process would take time. But as the days and weeks passed, the people began to find solace in their faith and in each other.

Churches played a central role in the healing process in towns and cities nationwide. Clergy from all denominations worked tirelessly to support their communities, offering counseling, organizing relief efforts, and providing hope in times of uncertainty. Congregations swelled as people returned to their faith, seeking comfort and guidance in the aftermath of the conflict.

Brother Michael, a minister in the Church of Christ who had been a beacon of light during the darkest days of the occupation, spoke to his congregation on the eve of the National Day of Prayer. "**We have been through a great trial**," he said, his voice filled with emotion. "**But we have emerged stronger, not because of our strength, but because we placed our trust in God. Let us now commit ourselves to living according to His will, loving our neighbors, and building a nation that reflects His glory.**"

The congregation, many of whom had lost loved ones in the war, found comfort in Father Michael's words. They knew the path to healing would not be easy, but they were ready to walk it together, guided by their faith and the knowledge that they were part of something greater than themselves.

Rebuilding with Purpose:

As the nation began rebuilding, the focus was not just on restoring what had been lost but on creating a better, more just society. The leadership of New America, guided by a renewed sense of purpose and faith, implemented policies that emphasized equality, justice, and the common good. The economy was rebuilt based on ethical principles, emphasizing supporting families, communities, and small businesses.

The military, which had played such a crucial role in the victory, was restructured to reflect the values of the new America. The emphasis was placed on defenses and peacekeeping, with a commitment to protecting the nation without resorting to unnecessary aggression. The soldiers who had fought bravely were honored with medals and ceremonies and tangible support—education, healthcare, and opportunities to build new lives in the country they had fought to protect.

However, the most significant change was in people's hearts and minds. There was a renewed sense of unity, recognizing that they were all together, regardless of their differences. The divisions that had once threatened to tear the nation apart began to heal, replaced by a spirit of cooperation and mutual respect.

A Vision for the Future:

As the National Day of Prayer approached, James Alexander addressed the nation in a televised speech broadcast to every home, military base, and gathering place.

"**My fellow Americans**," he began, his voice filled with conviction, "**we have come through a time of great trial and suffering. But we have emerged stronger, more united, and more faithful than ever. Our nation is whole again, not just in territory but in spirit. We are one people, under one flag, with one shared destiny.**"

He paused, allowing the weight of his words to settle in. "**But our journey is not over. We face many challenges, and the road ahead will not be easy. But I believe, with all my heart, that we will overcome these challenges, just as we have overcome past trials. We will rebuild our cities, our communities, and our lives. And we will do so with a renewed commitment to the values that have always made this nation great—freedom, justice, and faith in God.**"

Alexander's speech was met with overwhelming support. Across the country, people gathered in homes, churches, and public squares to watch and listen. His words resonated deeply with a nation that had been through so much and was now ready to move forward, united and determined to build a better future.

The National Day of Prayer:

When the National Day of Prayer finally arrived, it was like no other in American history. From coast to coast, Americans of all faiths and backgrounds came together to give thanks, to pray for the future, and to rededicate themselves to the principles that had guided their forefathers.

In Washington, D.C., a massive gathering occurred on the National Mall. Tens of thousands knelt in prayer, led by religious leaders from every denomination. The sight of many people united in faith and purpose was a powerful symbol of the nation's rebirth.

As the prayers rose to the heavens, a sense of peace settled over the crowd—a feeling!

Don't miss out!

Visit the website below and you can sign up to receive emails whenever William Myers publishes a new book. There's no charge and no obligation.

https://books2read.com/r/B-A-WBFNB-ONCXE

BOOKS2READ

Connecting independent readers to independent writers.

Did you love *A New Dawn*? Then you should read *The End of America Volume 2* by William Myers!

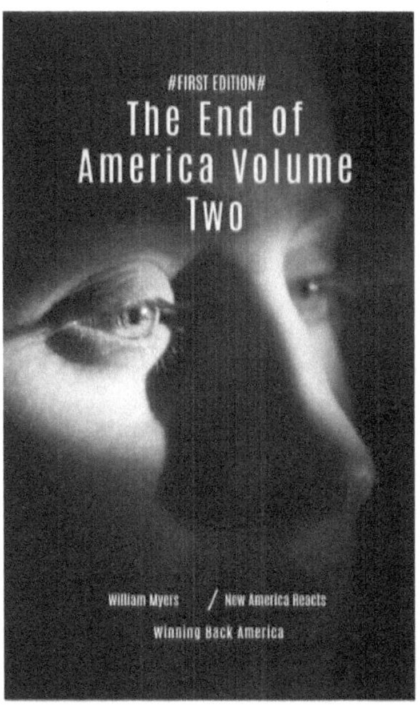

Volume 2 focuses on New America's plan to win back the other 30 states taken over by the enemy.

Read more at pauldingchurchofchrist.com.

About the Author

William has been a minister for 42 years. He has served congregations in Virginia, Tennssee, Indiana, California, North Dakota, and Ohio. He holds 4 undergraduate degrees and three graduate degrees. He has authored several books, and views his wife, Brenda, as his greatest supporter.

Read more at pauldingchurchofchrist.com.

www.ingramcontent.com/pod-product-compliance
Lightning Source LLC
Chambersburg PA
CBHW031428150726
47989CB00002B/857